THE
LAST
THING I
REMEMBER

Deborah Bee studied fashion journalism at Central St Martins. She has worked at various magazines and newspapers including *Vogue*, *Cosmopolitan*, *The Times* and the *Guardian* as a writer, a fashion editor and later an editor. Currently, she is a director of creative marketing in luxury retail.

THE LAST THING I REMEMBER

DEBORAH BEE

twenty7

First published in 2016 by Twenty7 Books

This paperback edition published in 2016 by

Twenty7 Books
80–81 Wimpole St, London W1G 9RE
www.twenty7books.com

A CIP catalogue record for this book is available from the British Library.

Paperback ISBN: 978-1-78577-020-3
Ebook ISBN: 978-1-78577-019-7

1 3 5 7 9 10 8 6 4 2

Printed and bound by Clays Ltd, St Ives Plc

Twenty7 Books is an imprint of Bonnier Zaffre,
a Bonnier Publishing company
www.bonnierzaffre.co.uk

For Felicity Green

1

Sarah

Day Zero – 11 p.m.

Hello. Hello?
  Can you hear me?
  Hello? I'm here.
  'Alright, Lisa?' A man's voice.
  I'm not Lisa. Am I? Am I called Lisa? What's my name?
  Hello?
  There's the sound of an engine switching off and running footsteps.
  'Another day in paradise, Tom. What you got?'
  That's a woman talking. She is out of breath.
  'Brain trauma. Female. Late twenties.'
  He sounds Australian. There is shouting in the background and more running. And a siren.
  'Tottenham?'
  'Yeah, Haringey.'
  'Evening, Lisa.'

Another male voice. Not Australian. More London.

'The one from White Hart Lane. We should keep a squad up there permanently on standby.'

There's the sound of scraping and clanking. Their voices are getting lost in the distance, cut short by gusts of wind.

'Thanks, Matt. We'll take her from here.'

'She say anything, Tom, did she? On the way. Did she, you know …?'

That's the London man.

'Nah, mate. She didn't say anything. I didn't say anything about anything else either. Usual procedure. Best leave that sort of stuff to the experts. You know.'

'She's not even conscious, is she?'

That was the woman again.

'No … Hang on a minute – she did say something.'

That's the first guy again. The Australian one.

'Well? What'd she say?'

'She said thank you'

'She did?'

Everything is quiet, apart from the traffic and the restless wind. Footsteps. Running. Someone arrives, breathing hard.

'Come on. The trauma unit is ready.'

'Can I just get that down on the report? So, she *was* conscious when you arrived on the scene?'

'She was then. We sedated her of course but, yes, at the scene she was conscious, just for a bit.'

'And she said thank you?'

'Yeah, Matt. "Thank you" – that's all she said.'

'What'd she say thank you for?'

'I dunno. She's British. The Brits always say thank you.'

Hello.

Hello?

Where've they gone?

This is me thinking.

I have woken up and I'm not there.

I can hear. There is a buzzing sound and a rhythmic heaving, in out in out, and a click, click, click, click.

But there is no me.

My body has gone.

I have disappeared.

This is me thinking.

That is all I can do.

I am a thought, lost in a dark, empty room, forgotten in an abandoned house.

It's dark. Too dark. Nothing but darkness.

Hello?

There are voices next to me. There's a clanking sound of metal hitting metal. People are straining to lift.

'Bed 4. Cerebral haemorrhage.'

'What time d'ya get home last night?'

Can you hear me? There are two women's voices. Close to me. I can hear them breathing.

'Quarter to five.'

'Same.'

'Can you do the admit for A&E?'

'Nah. I hate that fucking computer.'

'I've got Malin coming in ten. He's in early. Just my luck.'

'They haven't done the admit already, have they?'

'She only got here five minutes ago.'

'Don't tell me, Lisa's on.'

Lisa again. Is my name Lisa?

'How did you guess? Did you see Mark last night?'

'What, shit-faced and all over Emily?'

'Emily Whiting? Shut up. I didn't see that. Suspected brain haemorrhage, it says here. No life signs.'

'Really? Stroke?'

'No, mugged. Trauma to the anterior cranium. Tottenham. Not even that late. Brought in at ... 23:04. Been trying to stabilise her.'

'Really? Tottenham. Totally wrong nails for Tottenham.'

A door opens.

'I'm off, ladies. How was last night?'

'Yeah, Lisa, amazing. Have you done the admin for Bed 4?'

'I've been in A&E. Was Mark there?'

'I never saw him. Did you, Beth?'

'Who?'

'Mark.'

'Did you even make a start on the admit for Bed 4?'

'I brought her in – the preliminary report is right there. See you tomorrow ... bright and early.'

The door bangs.

'... when we will still be filling out this fucking form. She is such a lazy slag. I am so not surprised Mark dumped her.'

The door opens again.

'Beth. There's a man here to see Sarah.'

'Tell him no way. Jesus. Give us a chance. Who is he?'

'Brother.'

'Tell him no way. Not right now. Tell him we need to get her sorted. Take his number or something. Tell him, oh I don't know, tell him we'll call him. In a few hours.'

Hello. Can you hear me?

I have heard this voice before.

'Hello, Sarah.'

Sarah? Am I Sarah?

'Time to wake up now, Sarah. You're in hospital. I'm Nurse Hodder. You can call me Beth. I am one of the nurses looking after you. You've been in an accident and you are going to be fine. It's time to wake up now, Sarah. Can you hear me?'

Yes. YES, I CAN HEAR YOU.

CAN YOU HEAR ME?

None of this makes sense.

An accident?

I don't know why I am here. I don't know who I am. I'm not here. This isn't happening.

2

Kelly

You don't know me. I'm not what you think. You're just like all those people out there who think you can take one look at a person and, like, sum them up. Just like that. Just by the clothes they're wearing or the amount of lip gloss they've got on. I don't do that. I don't assume. That lady there, for example, in that orange plastic armchair in the corner, with the perm and the peach-coloured lipstick? You could look at her and think, middle-aged, middle-class, boring, watches *MasterChef* and listens to like Classic FM or something. Look at the tiny piece of pink toilet roll that she's dabbing her eyes with. It's twisted so tight. Someone my age, someone young, might decide that that lady didn't have much to fucking say that could interest me.

Drug smuggler. Seriously. She's a drug smuggler. The police were just talking to her. She's been brought from a maximum-security prison because her son has OD'd. He's on life support. You see, you don't know. I nearly shat myself when the nurse told me. I was like, OMG. You can't tell stuff just because her skirt's like this massive great tent. You have to see 'beyond the clothes' – that's what Sarah says. That's how this all works.

I look at how someone sits. You can tell a lot about a person by how they sit. How comfortable they look. Her arms are folded too tightly around her body – do you see? She's crossed her legs and the way that her foot is twisted and jammed behind her flesh-coloured support tights like my mum wears, that shows how nervous she is. How intimidated. Every time a policeman walks past the window she grips herself tighter. Every time the swing doors bang against the wall making the windows rattle in their dodgy wooden frames, she jumps and her eyes flick side-ways. Those things you can't control. They're much harder to mask than, say, how you put on a hairband or tie your tie. You need to really work at them.

You might think you can tell a lot about me just by looking at me, but you can't. You might think, yeah, she's around thirteen, maybe younger. She's a total geek. My skirt is the wrong length and my Little-Miss-Prim white shirt is overly white and beyond ironed. The collar lies nice and flat and my tie is neatly knot-ted. And this god-awful satchel. Totally random, I know. You think that makes me a type. My school socks are too long, folded over twice at the knee; my heels are sensible, beyond sensible – lace-ups. What sad fucker wears lace-ups? Even little kids don't wear lace-ups any more. You probably look at me and think I'm a bit sad. Maybe you feel a bit sorry for me. You think, bit of warpaint, bit of lipstick and mascara, and take off those goofy glasses, I might be sort of pretty. 'Your hair,' my Mum said to me the other day, while looking totally disappointed at my care-fully combed bunches. 'Your hair. D'ya think it could do with a bit of curl?' A bit of curl? It needs straightening irons and a pot of peroxide. Bunches at fourteen. That is actually sad. But, you'd think, bunches? Typical of a *nice* girl. A good girl. Sweet. She won't know anything about anything. She's probably so busy doing her homework or reading a fucking Jane Austen novel to even notice what's going on.

So, here I am. I'm in my school uniform because it was near-est my bed on my floor at 2 a.m. and I've been here for what, five hours. They came to Sarah's house in the middle of the night and then knocked on our door – we live next door. The blue flashing lights woke me up. I heard them ask if we knew Sarah. Asked if my mum was a good friend. She said yes. Slowly. Like she didn't want to hear what was gonna come next. They spoke real quiet so I couldn't hear. Then my mum saw me, standing at the top of the stairs, straining to hear in my PJs. My mum said I had to get dressed, then she went round and got Anna to look after Billy and we drove straight to the hospital. We waited here for like ages and they didn't say nothing to us. Not at all. My mum went home at six to get Billy ready for school. Cos he's a lame-o. Can't even make a sandwich for himself. Can't even get his uniform on. I bet I could get my fucking uniform on when I was fucking seven. She should've got back here again by now. She should be here any minute. She said she'd be really quick.

This is what they call the Family Room. It's got a sign on the door saying 'Family Room'. It's not really a sign. It's a bit of paper stuck with Sellotape that's gone yellow and split. Someone has made the sign with that clip-art software we have at school to make the title pages for our coursework projects. They've done it in like curly font, in the shape of a rainbow. Trying to kid you this is not totally a shit place to be. Patronising prettiness. It don't make it any better. This is where they park the visitors of people who are dying. You can come in any time – they don't have visiting hours for patients who are like really, really ill. The room is part of the Critical Care ward. That's what they call it when you are like really bad. There are windows running the side of one wall that let you see the corridor, who's going in and who's going out. And let whoever's in the corridor see you. From my seat right by the door I can lean my head out and see all the way down beyond the Family Room towards the wards. It's dark. The nurses' station is lit with like angle lamps and computer screens. They talk quiet. The phone rings a lot. There's like a hum of electricity. Beeping and clicking. And every so often the doors to the ward crash open as a trolley gets pushed through followed by policemen in hi-vis jackets and nurses carrying bags of water with tubes and stuff.

No one has really said anything to me. When we arrived a nurse just took our names and told us to wait. They wrote our names down on a list on a clipboard. They said we weren't relatives so we shouldn't be here at all. But then someone else, another nurse – older – checked the list and said we were OK because none of the relatives were here yet. Apart from some bloke who had come and gone and didn't even leave a name.

Do you know what I think? I think they thought she was gonna die. I'm not even lying. So they needed us here to identify her or something. They want you for filling out forms even if you're not related. I hate the police. Pigs.

And now, I don't fucking believe it, my mum's gone and I'm sitting here on my fucking own, right on the edge of this fucking plastic seat because if she dies I'll have to look at her body dead. I keep pushing my bum back into the chair but it doesn't feel right to be comfortable. The hot-water urn is bubbling in the corner next to a tray of like really horrible mismatched mugs standing in rings of washing-up foam and a box of sugar cubes that has got damp at some point at the bottom and so the cardboard has gone lumpy and torn. What'd they put them on there for anyway? Tea seems like too fucking comfortable when people next door are like dying. The lady in the corner looks too small in that great big armchair. She's still twisting that fucking tissue. Can't someone give her another one?

An old guy arrived at seven. He's parked in the corridor with the clipboard. He's just sat there. Old. Like maybe he volunteers or something. When a visitor buzzes the door he hauls himself up. He asks for a name then reads down his list. You can see people getting impatient. They think he is doing it too slow but they have to wait and be polite, while looking over his shoulder. Almost afraid to look over his shoulder. Then while he's still looking up and down the board, they might turn and look at me and the psycho in the Family Room. Some of them give me a bit of a smile. That's their sympathy smile. As if to say, there's a poor nice girl whose relative must be about to snuff it. What's she doing there all on her own? And then they head towards the nurses' station and their own relative hanging on to life by their fucking fingertips. Two more policemen come through the doors. Tinny shouting comes out of their radios. They look at the drug smuggler first, then at me. They check the list. They nod. They obviously think that I'll have nothing much to say. I look like the sort of girl who has nothing much to say. They continue to the wards. To Sarah. In a coma. Did I tell you that? The nurse says she's in a coma.

This wasn't supposed to happen.

3

Sarah

Day One – 8 a.m.

Hello?

Can you hear me now?

'Morning. Are you Mum?'

Mum? A woman's voice answers quietly – almost whispers. It's a thin voice.

'Yes, I'm her mother. This is Brian. He's Dad.'

'How are you both? Was it a long drive you had?'

'It was more the shock, wasn't it, Brian?'

There is a constant beeping sound and intermittent clicks. Her voice feels a long way off even though she must be close.

'So,' *Lucinda – she's the Irish one,* 'can I ask you a few questions about Sarah, now that you both have your tea?'

There's the sound of papers being leafed through.

'Did you fill out this form with Nurse Hodder outside? The ones about Sarah's age and occupation, all that?'

'Yes, nurse. We did that when we got here. Sarah's twenty-eight. She's always been a good girl.'

She's starting to cry.

'She's never been in any trouble.'

'D'ya know what? I think everything is complete here. Let me go and check. So how are we doing with our talking, Mum? Have we been trying to talk to Sarah, like Nurse Hodder said? Did Nurse Hodder explain?'

She's shouting a bit.

'Oh yes. We've talked to her, haven't we, Brian? Brian! He hasn't got his hearing aid in. He didn't even have time to pick it up. They came, you know. In the night. The police did. He didn't hear the door. He never hears the door. The only reason I heard it was because I've had this cough and I'd got up to make a cup of coffee. I find a coffee sends me off. Just a small cup and then, twenty minutes later, I'm out. Gone. The kitchen is right next to the front door, you see. It overlooks our drive.

'Actually it was the blue lights that I saw first. I thought they'd come for that boy again down on the corner. He's nothing but trouble to his parents since he left school. But the police car came all the way down to our end. Woke the whole road, I shouldn't wonder. They'll think we're common criminals.

'They didn't put the siren on. They don't put the siren on for domestic situations, that's what the young man told us, unless there's violence, you see. But they do put the blue light on if it's an emergency. And this is an emergency because they're just not sure that, well ... you know. They said they weren't sure.

'Took us three hours to get here. In the dark. We don't know the area. Don't know it at all. Not even in the light, you see. So they said they would give us a lift. That was kind. I thought the government didn't have any money. Wasn't it kind, though? I could see Paul, you know, he's Rachel's husband, on the corner looking out of his lounge window from behind the new vertical louvre blinds they've just had fitted. I would have waved to show that we didn't have those restraints on, you know. Handcuffs. But I was too busy looking for Brian's glasses in my handbag.

'We'd just put on what clothes we had out, you see. I don't think you'll mind me saying that I'm actually wearing what I had on yesterday. Well, you see, it's an emergency, isn't it? And I just picked up my handbag. My glasses were in there from last night, when we were at Jean's for the rummy night. We go every week for the rummy. Since her John died. But anyway I haven't got Brian's glasses. He'd taken his out the night before, you see, to look at the paper. He likes to read a bit before he goes off, you know. So his glasses will still be on the bedside table.

'Do you know, Lucinda, you could say anything about him right now and he wouldn't hear a word. Not a word.'

'Morning there, Dad.'

The Irish girl is still shouting.

'Have you been trying to talk to Sarah, Dad? We know how helpful it is, don't we?'

'We have. Haven't we, June? Oh yes.'

'Would you like some tissues, Mr Beresford? Mr Beresford? I have some super-mansized tissues here.'

Dad.

Is that my dad?

He is crying.

These people here in this room, they can see me. They can't hear me. Hello?

I'm here. HELLO!

I can't open my eyes. I can't move my hands. I can't feel my body. It's like I'm here but I'm not here. I've lost myself.

Coma. That's what this is. This is a coma from the inside. Coma. I'm opening the eyes inside my head. As wide as I can. Everything is black. It's blacker than black. Like inside a coal mine. I've been inside a coal mine. I remember a thick yellow gate smeared with black dust, banging shut. The clanking of a lift as it's swinging downwards. They told us that in a coal mine it is blacker than black. And it was. Not even a glimmer of light from anywhere.

There is no light here. Just sound. It's like I've been buried in a hole and covered over.

I'm dying then.

Dying.

I thought they said when you die, you see a tunnel of light. I'm supposed to see a light and I walk towards it and then I find God, surrounded by distant family members who I don't recognise. But they recognise me. They hug me. It's like being at a wedding. Or a funeral.

There's no light.

There's nothing.

I'm not surprised.

I'd be more surprised if there was.
I don't think I'm a God fan.
Am I?
This can't be happening.

4

Kelly

Day One – 8 a.m.

Still here. Still waiting. The pigs in hi-vis jackets come and go. Visitors sign in with the old guy. The drug smuggler is out cold. The scrunched-up tissue is drying out, in the palm of her open hand. But still no one has said anything more about Sarah. Maybe they've forgotten about me.

If they could've seen me back when I was twelve – or like nearly twelve – they would've thought something else, something quite different. They'd have noticed me then. You would have too. If you'd seen me walking home from school, socks rolled down, scuffed up platforms, dyed blond hair, Rimmel Scandaleyes blue waterproof eyeliner. My blazer collar would be up at the back like the girls in Year 13. I had quite a cool bag back then. Got it in Wood Green market – looked exactly like Prada, though. Same gold lettering and everything. Wonder where that's got to now. When Billy started at the junior school, Mum said I had to collect him and get him home safely. Hold his hand all the way.

He was five. He's seven now, and a right royal pain – that's what my mum always says. But he's alright, if you tell him he is. Once he knows not to do something, he don't do it. He knows now not to touch my stuff. Not never. Don't go in my room. Not never. Don't tell Mum nothing. He's alright. So there was this one day, when he was doing what he was told, holding my hand like I'd said, like Mum had said, and it was a sunny afternoon. Actually, really sunny. The pavement was fucking boiling. The tarmac on the road had gone shiny at the edges, like where it was melting. We were loping along even slower than usual. I mean you never walk fast coming back from school, do you, but sometimes it would take us three times as long as it takes to get there in the mornings. Even longer on hot days like that one. We'd stopped off at Tesco Express to get sweets. We always did. Mum doesn't know that. We used our dinner money. Sometimes we'd have to wait to get in because only four kids are allowed in at any one time. It says so on the door. It says 'South Haringey Primary and Secondary Schools – 4 children only at ANY ONE TIME' – that last bit's written in thick black magic marker. Obviously it didn't actually say that they suspected the kids of stealing, shoplifting, but everyone who saw the notice knew what it meant. We were really pissed off when it first went up. My mum told the Tesco people off and wrote in to the school. Mrs Backhouse wrote an official letter and complained that our schools were being sin- gled out unfairly. The Tesco people wrote an official letter back saying that all the children were in a grey and navy uniform with a South Haringey tie. Plus there aren't any other schools nearby so it had to be us. In fairness it *was* us, but it might not have been, right? Despite keeping the numbers to a manageable four, and putting up cameras and mirrors in all four corners of the store, Tesco Express in White Hart Lane didn't get any less shoplifting. We just got better at it. It was a game. We'd just wait until one of the staff went out the back. Or a few customers were at the counter. Then strike. Sometimes one of us would distract one of them – by asking if they had any salad cream or something difficult to find, and then when they went to look for it we would fill up our pockets with Haribo sours. Billy didn't do it. He was too young back then. He'd probably do it now if I let him. But I don't even do that stuff now. I'm good. Like I said earlier … now, I talk nice and dress like a goon.

We'd already got our sweets that day. Billy's got a drumstick lolly with the pink and yellow wrapper – he still loves them. And I'd got my prawn cocktail crisps. I prefer smoky bacon flavour now. I go through phases with crisps. But I remember wishing I'd chosen something else cos eating prawn cocktail crisps and holding Billy's hand was totally rank. I had to keep dropping his hand so I can get the crisps out of the pack and then lick the pink stuff off my fingers and quickly pick up his hand again, in case Mum caught me, or one of her neighbours saw. She knows just about everyone in the street. And his hand was hot and sweaty and tacky from holding the lolly stick, and sometimes when I licked off the prawn cocktail pink stuff from my own hand I got a bit of the taste of his drumstick. We'd got nearly to the last corner before our street, and Billy was chattering away like always. And smiling. And I was laughing at something he said about Miss Treneer, who he always used to get wrong and called Miss Trinnier. And then suddenly, out of nowhere, I yanked his arm. Like really hard. Like nearly out of his socket, hard. Poor Billy. He was so shocked. He had no idea what was going on. One minute laughing, next minute he was crying hard. Screaming. So what am I? A psycho in the making, you think? If you could pull back from the scene a bit then you'd have seen what was going on. On the other side of the road, that bloke who had just come around the bend, in the hoody, with the funny rolling way of walking, that was Wino, aka Joe Herne. They say he walks like that cos he's pissed all the time but I don't really think so. Mum said he was born that way – with a funny hip. She used to know his mum. She had another kid who had something wrong with it too. Autistic or something. But really bad. But that's not the sort of thing you want to get caught talking about. Wino would kill you for talking about that. He lives on the Huntley Estate, still with his mum. If he lives there, you wouldn't think he'd be able to afford to be pissed on wine all the time. Most of his mates drink lager. To start with everyone thought he was a complete girl for not drinking lager and drinking wine instead but nobody would say that now. Nobody would say anything, to Wino or about Wino. He's Year 10. Kathryn Cowell's year. Kathryn Cowell's best mate. Kathryn Cowell's henchman.

Pulling Billy's arm out of his socket, almost, may seem like a random thing to do just because Wino is on the other side of the road, right? But I had to do something fast. Having a laughing little kid brother was like a chink in your armour – something else to screw you over with. Acting like you didn't care about nothing was how you got through South Haringey Secondary. It was bully or get bullied, right? You had to act hard or you'd get picked on – but not too hard, or you'd be competition. If you acted tough you would look like you belonged, that you approved, that you were one of them. So that's what we all did. Not just me. All my friends did the same. We dressed hard, we acted hard. If their crew was around, you just jutted out your chin a bit and set your mouth in a thin-lipped grimace, never met their eyes, and then you were in the crowd. That was the idea. Anyone looking vaguely vulnerable or scared would get robbed. Anyone showing off their new phone, robbed. Anyone daft enough to carry a laptop, robbed. People who stood out, they'd lose their dinner money, mobile, earrings, packed lunch – whatever it was you were carrying that Kathryn decided she wanted. She took someone's puppy once. But they did get it back – their dad went round her mum's. Maybe dinner money was how Wino funded his alco habit. Dinner money goes a long way when you've robbed twenty kids in one day. After I got onto Wino's radar, there was no going back. Every time he saw me he'd wrap his hand around my ponytail and yank my head back. ''Ello, Blondie. What you got?' That's when my mum was starting to get suspicious, given the black eye and the bruises. But nothing was gonna get that out of me. Some things have to be kept secret. Best not to fucking say anything.

So, anyway, when we'd got to that corner and Wino was out of sight, my mum, in her slippers and her apron, came racing out of the house, where she'd been twitching her nets at the front window waiting for us. And she picked Billy up and cuddled him and he was still crying and chewing his drumstick lolly at the same time, and there was a line of sticky pink and yellow dribble coming out of the corner of his mouth and draining onto Mum's white crochet cardigan and I said, 'Mum, he just tripped. He's fine', and he nodded silently, his face half hidden by her steel-grey perm. And she carried him into the kitchen and put him on his naff little stool where his squash was waiting, in his favourite naff Spiderman cup, and his small plate of biscuits was right next to it. And I looked in the hall mirror and applied another layer of glittery lip gloss in Pepto-Bismol pink, looking like the sort of girl who has a lot to say.

Fuck. I wonder where my mum has got to. How long can it take to get Billy to school? He's such a dick.

This all happened before my re-education. This is before I was taken in hand and restyled and reformed, and turned into the sort of girl who doesn't get noticed. Because Sarah said it's better not to get noticed at all than get noticed for the wrong things. She said if you're going to pretend to be something you're not, better to pretend to be nothing. Then you won't get seen. Then you disappear. That's what she said. And she said looking like a bit of a loser would make me disappear off Kathryn Cowell's radar, and anyone else's for that matter. She said I could become invisible.

You're probably thinking that this is really random because it's all happening in the wrong order. Twelve-year-old girls are supposed to be girly and do-gooding, then, bang, hit thirteen and become monsters. This is mainly right. All the girls at school did that, even Samantha Elliott who was seriously a total twat until she came back after the summer holidays with blond highlights. If you flicked back to when I was, say, ten you'd have seen the makings of the prissy self you see here today. At ten I wasn't allowed to dye my hair yet. Mum had let me get my ears pierced when I was eight and I got my belly button done when I was eleven but Auntie Liz took me and Mum still doesn't know. If I'm honest it was a bit rank. It's healed up now. It went septic after a week and I seriously thought I was going to die because I was never going to tell Mum what I'd done because she'd have literally killed me, and all this yellow stuff started coming out. I'm not even lying. Auntie Liz took me down the doctors and they gave me some special talcum, and some tablets that I had to hide in my Rice Krispies.

Also when I was eleven I got my highlights done for the first time. It was my last year at junior school. Auntie Liz took me down the salon in Haringey High Road for a half-head and I got to sit on like three cushions so I could see myself in the mirror. My mum said it looked quite nice, but it wasn't really blond enough so I spent my Christmas money on getting a full set and went for White Platinum rather than Golden Glow and it looked wicked. Clare Millard in my class had had hers done there too and had the White Platinum as well so we looked the same. Like twins. Everyone said we actually were twins. We got the same wedge shoes too. And the same glittery lip gloss in Pepto-Bismol pink. And when we went out together people used to look at us and point. My mum said it didn't look nice. Not at all. She got really angry. I got the 'shabby little tart' line. But it was too late. By the time I turned twelve, I had the complete shabby-little-tart look down to an art.

The transformation from shabby little tart back to loser was not my idea. I'm not that smart. Well, I wasn't back then. It didn't happen overnight either, but it was a conscious gradual toning down of everything, from my hair – back to mousy – to my make-up – none – to my uniform looking boring. Probably at first I didn't even know she was doing it. As I say, it wasn't even my idea. It was Sarah's. And now she's going to die. Fucking brilliant.

5

Sarah

Day One – 9 a.m.

'Mr and Mrs Beresford? Yes? Uh huh? Good. Mr and Mrs Beresford.'

He sounds very official.

'Thank you for coming so quickly. I understand you all had quite a drive this morning.'

'It wasn't really morning, was it, Brian? It was the middle of the night.'

'Winchester, is it? Lovely part of the world. So, Mr and Mrs Beresford, I am *sorry* for these difficult circumstances. We are *all* so sorry. I think the best thing that I can do is explain exactly what has happened to Sarah here so that you can understand what we are doing. Has anyone explained to you exactly what has happened here? Right, right, I thought not. Alright, good, uh huh, well, Sarah has suffered what we call a cerebral haemorrhage …'

Cerebral haemorrhage? Someone has started crying.

'... caused by trauma to the brain. The bruising to the face and the swelling around the eyes indicates that the force of the blow was sufficient to rupture blood vessels. You understand that the impact of hitting the pavement ...'

What pavement?

'... the probable impact – this is still with the police, you understand – during the assault caused a fracture to the skull. In this situation we might have expected there to be an extra-axial haemorrhage – that's a haemorrhage on the outside of the brain. In fact, what we believe we have here is an intra-axial haemorrhage ...'

Intra-axial? Is that good? It sounds bad. Is it better than an extra-axial whatever?

'I don't think we really understand what you're saying, um, doctor.'

That's the one they keep calling 'Mum'. She doesn't sound familiar.

'... in other words it is within the brain tissue. We often see these in stroke victims, where the pressure has built up and built up. For Sarah it was caused by a sudden blow to the skull. The skull is fractured, but the intracranial pressure has not decreased. The brain is swelling, dangerously. When she came in last night we put her into what is called an induced coma – to give her brain a rest.'

Swelling dangerously!

There is more crying and the sound of a nose being blown.

'Sarah isn't the sort of girl who ever got mixed up in this kind of thing, doctor.'

The doctor's voice becomes too low to hear.

Mr and Mrs Beresford. So they are my parents. I have parents. And my name is Sarah Beresford. It doesn't sound familiar at all, Sarah Beresford. What would sound like me?

'... I'm afraid so. The mortality rate for intraparenchymal bleeds is over 40 per cent.'

Does anyone actually know what he is talking about? I don't.

'The treatment that we advise for this type of trauma is sedation. For the first few hours we keep the sedation high to give the brain time to recover, then we start to gradually reduce it so that we can see what damage has been done. We've already started to bring that down. We want to see if it's possible for Sarah to reach a conscious state. Do you see? Sarah will continue to be assisted with her breathing through this tube here. She will be fed through this tube. Her sedation is administered up here. So for the next few days we will continue to monitor her progress and look for signs.'

'How long will she be like this, doctor?'

'Mrs Beresford, I can't really answer that. The brain is very complicated. Generally we say that we'll have a very good idea of the future for brain trauma in ten days. But in truth we don't know much. We have to look for signs of any brain activity. What sometimes happens in this kind of situation, and I'll put this in simple terms, is that the brain forgets how to do things. You know, like breathe, or swallow.'

'What? The brain forgets to breathe. How long for?'

That was my dad, I think.

'For some patients it's short term. Others aren't so lucky. They have a long-term disability, I'm afraid. But it's too early for us to say that in this case.'

'What, so, when she wakes up, she might end up in a wheelchair, is that what you mean?'

Yes, is that what you mean?

'I'm not going to lie to you, Mr Beresford. There's quite a catalogue of possible damage: there's personality changes, impaired sensation, paralysis, incontinence, visual or language problems, deafness, blindness, seizures, even swallowing difficulties and neurological deficits.'

'Neurological deficits?'

Neurological deficits.

'Yes – that's right. Whatever the brain can't remember needs to be retaught. New channels have to be made from A to B. It may be like starting all over again. Do you see? If we were to see some movement in Sarah – anything at all, a twitch of her hand or anything – we would know that there are some old channels left or some new channels being made, that some messages are getting through.'

'Getting through?'

'Yes, uh huh, Mrs Beresford. Getting through. Channels. If you could keep chatting to Sarah and reminding her of special times from her childhood, you know, birthdays or holidays, maybe a party or a trip somewhere – that might just trigger her memory and pull her out of it.'

'So can she hear us then, doctor, is that what you're saying?'

'There's a possibility, Mr Beresford, that Sarah has what we call locked-in syndrome. She could be listening to everything we're saying.'

Dad, I can hear you. DAD!

A door clicks shut. There's the sound of scraping chairs. It's gone quiet, apart from the hum of the equipment. And some sniffing.

'Brian?'

'What is it, love?'

'Is mortality rate the dying rate or the staying-alive rate?'

I can hear you, Dad.

DAD!

I'm in here.

I can't get out.

This is bad. All I can actually do is hear. Oh, and think. I suppose you can count that, right? I am here and I can hear, so I do not have neurological deficits. If I try really hard I could open my eyes. I must be able to. I can maybe move my nose. It's not that far from my brain to my nose, is it? A shorter journey. Gotta be easier than, say, like, all the way to my big toe. OK, I'll try twitching a toe. OK, a finger is nearer.

I'm tired.

It's dark.

I'm stretching my fingers out but I can't find a door.

I'm screaming but no one can hear.

6

Kelly

Day One – 9 a.m.

For fuck's sake. My mum still isn't back, the drug smuggler's still in the corner and the mugs still have foam around them. Who knew that foam could last that long?

I would phone my mum but you're not allowed to use mobile phones in here. There are signs everywhere. Same clip-art rainbow writing. Someone must have had a good day on the computer. The signs say that mobiles can cause 'INTERFERENCE WITH THE HOSPITAL COMPUTER SYSTEMS'. There's a pink cartoon bear, frowning, with one hand on his hip and the other holding a mobile to his ear. He's standing like a totally gay bear. Why do they put cartoons on important messages? I mean, it makes perfect sense you don't want interference with life-support machines, right? But what's the bear got to do with it?

The police are here, like three of them in and out and, guess what, they are on their mobiles all the time. That's a fuck load of interference. No one asks them to turn them off.

I bet I could ring my mum without bringing down the entire fucking system, right?

When Sarah first moved into our street, my mum was so happy. I mean seriously. Totally. 'The yuppies are coming to Tottenham,' she told everyone. I'm not even lying. Anna – from like three along, she's Greek – she has her son and daughter-in-law and their daughter all living with her now and she's been relegated to the front bedroom because my mum says the daughter-in-law doesn't like her – she is the only person in the world not to know what a yuppie is. 'Posh people are coming to Tottenham,' my mum explained. She even told the postman.

By the time they actually arrived, I had decided to hate Sarah. My mum hadn't even met her and was fucking obsessed. The first time I actually saw her, she was getting out of a white car parked outside their house, which is right next door to ours. I told you that? She was wearing a beige jacket, like a posh biker jacket, and a white T-shirt and jeans. She had navy Converse – Low Tops – and her black hair was long then, and perfectly shiny – like in a TV commercial. She was perfectly perfect really. I have never seen anyone so pretty in real life. She was so pretty you just wanted to touch her. She seemed to have like golden light coming right out of her.

She's changed a lot in the last two years. Maybe it's just because I got to know her and, you know, saw that she wasn't really totally perfect. Maybe it's because she stopped wearing any make-up. But even scrubbed clean she still radiated something. Mind you, she didn't look the same with short hair. I don't know why she got her hair cut that short. Adam was furious. Did I tell you yet about Adam?

And she went thinner too. Her jeans didn't fit properly at the back. She used to say to me, 'Kelly, tell me the truth. Does my bum look big in these?' And at first her bum did look big but, you know, big in a good way. Like a normal bum. But one day when she said it, I realised that she didn't have a bum any more. I said to her, 'You don't have a bum any more, Sarah. Your legs just, like, meet your back', and she laughed and then looked in the mirror. And then she looked sad and she pulled down her sweater, over her bum like girls with big bums do.

What the fuck do you think she looks like now? They haven't let me see her yet. I've been here half the fucking night and they haven't said anything more to me.

It's like gone nine o'clock. Nine o'-fucking-clock and my eyes are on fucking fire. The traffic must be bad on Green Lanes. She could have come round the North Circular way but she won't, you know. She's so shit at driving. She will never go a different way to the one that she always goes. My mum is such a loser sometimes.

'Hello. Are you Kelly?'

A woman is sitting down next to me. She's one of those well-meaning types who smiles a cheesy smile even when a situation is like fucking terrible. She must've been a hippy. You know. She has those old-fashioned lace-up shoes on that look like Cornish pasties. That's what my mum calls them. They're purple. They look like they've been dyed with like fucking beetroots or something. Look, I'm sure she means well. It's just annoying when people try to fool you with niceness.

'Hi. Yes.' Smile back.

'You're a friend of Sarah's.' She consults her clipboard. 'Kelly, I'm Gill Brannon.' She looks me right in the eyes. I think that's supposed to make me feel like she's telling the truth or something. 'I'm what's called a victim support officer.' She says 'victim' and 'support' very slowly, like I'm deaf or a retard or something.

'She's my mum's friend, really,' I say. This isn't true, of course, but whatever a victim support officer is supposed to do, I can live without, right?

'I see, Kelly,' she writes something scribbly down on her pad.

'Well, I'm afraid there's not much you or your mum can do here at the moment. Sarah's family are here now. They arrived an hour or so ago and the doctor is seeing them. It was good of you and your mum to come in the middle of the night to support Sarah and I'm sure she will be very grateful for that, knowing that she had someone to be with her in case she needed that.'

She's nodding frantically as she speaks. What a nut job.

'To be honest, it's probably best for you to go home. Are you alright to get home? Will your mum pick you up? Sarah is in a stable but critical condition and I think you've done a great job.'

The drug smuggler in the corner is watching me.

'I have got some homework,' I say. As though that is relevant.

I pick up my satchel and put the tea mug I'd been holding next to the tray by the urn. The drug smuggler is following me under her fringe.

'My mum is just taking Billy to school, you see. She's coming back any minute. I think she just thought ...'

'Kelly, Sarah's not conscious now. Is that OK?'

What a daft bitch. No, it's not OK. Wake her up!

'Yes, I'll tell my mum. She'll come tomorrow.'

'Kelly ...'

I hate it when people keep saying your name. Why do they do that? What are they trying to prove?

'Kelly, could you possibly ask your mum to give me a call? Could you?' She presses a piece of paper in my hand. It's a pink piece of paper with her name and phone number photocopied onto it. She probably has a stack in her bag.

'Get her to call before she comes. We don't want her to waste a journey, do we? I'm sure your friend will be feeling better soon.'

'She's my mum's friend, really,' I say again, as though I have forgotten that I just said it.

We start to head towards the double doors.

'Bye, then,' I say to the drug smuggler in the corner, as we move between the rows of plastic chairs. (Don't you think that would make a totally awesome film title – 'The Drug Smuggler in the Corner'?) She looks away. Beaten. I smile. 'Hope your son feels better soon.'

It's so fucking funny when adults think you're totally stupid.

7

Sarah

Day One – 4 p.m.

'Hello, my beautiful girl.'

That's my dad. I remember my dad.

'Your mother's gone to get some tea. Someone's told her there's a tea trolley nearby. And you know your mother. She's never more than five minutes away from a cup of tea. I thought, you know ... while she's not here, you know. Look, I don't know if you can hear me, love. But if you can, you need to open your eyes now and come back to us. The doctor said you could hear. Well, he said maybe you could hear. So come on then. Show me you can hear me. Show me your beautiful hands. Flutter your lovely eyelashes. Remember your red slippers? Remember how you sat on my knee and learned how to tie a bow on them. Remember? Remember how the next day you could tie your dressing-gown belt?'

I do remember, Dad. I do. I remember a house with a yellow front door. The house was neat and regular like a picture-book house. There were two windows downstairs and two upstairs, symmetrically spaced out. All the windows had white net curtains behind them, not fancy festoony ones, just plain, patternless nylon that made the house look as though its eyes were half-closed, like it was a little bit shy. Running down the side of the house was a concrete drive. There was grass straining through cracks down the middle of it. And a brown car was waiting on it. A Mini Clubman with wooden bits around the windows. I remember sitting on your lap, Dad, holding the steering wheel in both hands and driving the car towards the garage. At least I thought that was what I was doing. And you would tell me, 'Watch the road, chicken.' You called me 'chicken'. Or 'flowerpot'. And if I had chocolate on my hands, or ice-cream that made my hot fingers stick together, you wouldn't mind. 'Watch the road, chicken,' you'd say. And I'd watch the road really hard as we slowly crept up the drive. And whenever I turned my head to look at you, there'd be a twinkle in your eye. We'd reach the wooden garage doors at the end of the drive and I'd stop. You would pull on the handbrake and lean forward to pull the door handle back. I'd jump off your lap and run down the garden, in and out of a line of thin pear trees that you'd only planted the year before. And you would whip your white hanky from your trouser pocket when you thought I wasn't looking and begin to rub away at the sugary fingerprints until the steering wheel gleamed again. Before my mum found out. The whole scene runs like an old-fashioned ciné film, tinged with golden sunshine, and buzzing with insects suspended in the air.

'Hello, my beautiful girl. Time to wake up now, my darling. We need you back. Can you hear me, Sarah? Can you come back?'

Dad, I think I've got lost.

DAD. I CAN'T FIND YOU.

'Afternoon, Mr Beresford. Still here? Afternoon, Sarah. Gosh, it's turned into a nasty day. Raining, raining, raining.'

I recognise her voice.

'It's time to get Sarah ready for the night shift, Mr Beresford. Is that OK?'

'Nurse, can I just ask you something? The doctor, earlier, he said ten days. Ten days. Is that normal for this kind of thing?'

'Yes, it is. But with brain injuries, it's so hard to be precise. We'll just have to wait and see.'

'Right. OK then. Well, goodbye, dear.'

That's my dad. He always calls everyone 'dear'.

'Goodbye, Mr Beresford. Chin up, eh?'

I hear the click of the door and then someone else arrives.

Another nurse. They are talking over me. Like I'm not here. Like I'm already dead. Lisa is late for her shift. Lisa is always late for her shift. Lisa is always on 'a massive diet'. Lisa is size 6.

'Did you see the way she showed us that Top Shop dress she bought but made sure the size tag was out so everyone could see it?'

'I don't care how thin she is, those leggings she wears are lewd.'

'What does lewd actually mean? Is it like the same as rude?'

'Yeah, but worse. Doesn't she wear *any* knickers? Those leggings go all the way up her arse.'

'Maybe she wears those cheese strings?'

'G-strings. I think cheese strings are something else. Have you seen her camel toe?'

'Oh my god? Really? She has camel's toes?'

'No, not a real camel toe. She doesn't actually have A CAMEL'S TOE! It's a saying, isn't it? That's just what they call it when you can see someone's fanny, you know, at the front. When it's going up their front bum. Camel toe.'

'Do they? Camel toe. That's hilarious. What's it called when you can see a man's bits?'

'Is it ... a nice view?'

They are both giggling. I am giggling. Cheese strings! I found something funny. Fuck neurological deficits. The door clicks open.

'Afternoon, Lisa. Nice of you to drop by.'

'How was Top Shop?'

'Shut up, Lucinda. I'm not even that late. I had to collect some stuff from stationery actually. Hi, Beth. Very nice, thanks. I got this great pair of leggings. I'll show you later.'

'Leggings, eh? Great.'

'How's she doing? Any change?'

'Too early to tell.'

'What happened then, do they know?'

'Just what they said before. Mugging, they think, that went wrong. That's what they said. Just wrong time, wrong place. Maybe someone interrupted them. Maybe the muggers got scared and lashed out. Imagine how she's gonna feel when she finds out her husband's dead. Maybe she'll wish she hadn't woken up.'

'We shouldn't talk about that in here, Lucinda, shut up. How many times do I have to remind you not to talk in front of patients. They may not look like they can hear. But don't you believe it. We've had plenty who've woken up and told us they heard everything.'

Husband. What husband? Everything has gone totally silent. There are no clicks, no beeps now. It's like someone turned the volume down.

Click.

Gone.

There is only black and silence.

I had a husband.

He is dead.

8

Kelly

Day One – 7 p.m.

As soon as I had got out of the ward, my mum was like belting down the hall towards me. If she walked at that speed all the time she wouldn't need to go to fucking pilates. I'm not even lying. She'd got her church coat on. She only wears that for Father O'Shea or for funerals. She'd missed her mouth with her lipstick. It was all over her fucking teeth.

'Jesus, Mary and Joseph, Kelly! Where the hell d'ya think you're going?' she'd yelled, but in that totally fierce whisper she saves for when we're out.

I told her we weren't allowed in. That Sarah's family was there now and that we had to ring. Ring Mrs Branston, or whatever her name was.

So we went home. She'd parked in the hospital multi-storey and once we'd found the car – she always manages to lose the fucking car – she'd talked all the way home.

About how Haringey didn't used to be so rough. About the danger of joining gangs. About how half my school were gonna get banged up any day soon. About how I'd be banged up too if I didn't start doing my homework. And I said that she was the one who put me in a waiting room for half the fucking night, so how was I supposed to do my fucking homework? And she said she wasn't meaning specifically that day, but in general and she said I fucking knew what she was fucking talking about so don't be so fucking clever and stop saying fucking all the time.

She said that they'd all been all over the local news. On breakfast TV. That it happened just by the Rec entrance – the Rec is the park down White Hart Lane. I knew that bit. It's where Kathryn Cowell hangs out with her homies. On the edge of the Rec there's a community centre – during the day they use it as a nursery and day-care centre for homeless people. Not at the same time obvs. In the evening they do adult-education stuff like CV writing and computer literacy for like really old people who don't know how to switch on their screens. Some of the teachers from school volunteer there. Sarah and I went there a few times. Quite a lot of times actually. That was just after I first met her. I'd come home with this fat black eye and when my mum asked me about it I said I just had an argument with my locker door – which was halfway true. She knew I was halfway lying. But it's not like I was gonna tell my mum what had happened. I mean, she's one of those mums who would be all over that. Marching down the school. Grabbing someone by the ear. Having a go at the headmistress. Fact is, no one could make any difference to how things were run at the school. That was clear. So my mum asked Sarah to have a chat with me about it. Sarah was posh, you see, in my mum's eyes. Since she'd moved in Sarah had become Mum's NBF. Mum was always hovering by the net curtains – not in a nosey way although obvs it was nosey. More in a helpful way. Like she'd take parcels in for them off the postman. Or have a spare Hoover bag. Or she'd race out to help Sarah with the shopping. Sarah was pretty and successful – she worked for some publishing company or something, and Anna down the road saw her bank statements one time, and she said that Sarah earned like shedloads of money. Well, not shedloads, but it was better than say working in like a shop or even as a waitress with tips. And I guess my mum thought I was heading for a shop or a cafe and not for A levels and university and a proper job with a proper wage. I suppose she thought that some of Sarah's poshness might rub off on me if she threw us together enough. And I guess she also thought I was some daft fucking twat who would open up to someone 'more your own age'. Favourite line of my mum's.

Which of course I did. Somehow Sarah understood right away. You know what, she didn't even ask me about that black eye. Smart, huh? She just knew. And you know most grown-ups, when you talk to them about bullying, they think that the answer is to do something about the bully. But you know what, Sarah didn't. 'You can't change people.' That's what she said. 'You can't change people, but you can change you.' So we did this self-esteem class, which sounds odd for a teenager and a successful young woman, but at the time we thought it would be a bit of a laugh and I think Sarah was just trying to get me to be a bit more confident, you know.

Anyhow, Sarah said we should try it once and if we didn't like it we didn't have to go back, did we? She said I didn't believe in myself enough. She said I'd spent too much time listening to conversations in hallways and worrying about stuff that wasn't even my fault and shooting my mouth off at school or jutting out my chin to be in the in crowd. And she said at my age I should be having fun, not getting my new Nokia with an HD camera nicked. At first, I definitely thought she was doing me this like massive favour coming with me. I mean, I was sure she had loads of like important stuff to be doing, like for work and shit. But when we turned up, she didn't pull that thing that grown-ups do, when they kind of talk over your head and pull faces, like they think you suddenly can't even fucking see that they're pulling faces. Sarah said I was her friend, and that we were coming together to find out more about the course. And the lady that ran it, Fleur she was called, which Sarah said is flower in French, which is like totally cool and if ever I have a baby girl, I shall call her Fleur cos it sounds posh. Anyway, she was just really nice, and so were the other ladies, apart from one, Belinda, who was just seriously nuts. So there were seven of us, eight if you include this Fleur woman. And we sat in a circle on these beige plastic chairs that had pen scribble on, and talked, and even though Sarah and I didn't say anything much, and it could've been totally embarrassing and everything, actually it wasn't. You had to say things like what your best friend meant to you. Obviously I talked about Clare. I told them how we had the same hair and the same lip gloss and the same platforms, so we looked like twins. And then you had to say what your best friend had that you didn't have. And the person you most admired in the world. Sarah said the person she most admired in the world was her sister, because she had the courage to speak out. And I said that my best friend was Clare and what she had that I didn't have was half my clothes and everybody laughed, which I thought was unfair to start with cos she did actually have half my fucking clothes but then, after I had blushed quite a bit, I realised that it was actually quite funny so I laughed too and then everyone else laughed more. Then they did this thing where you had to say what you saw when you looked in the mirror. Not just your reflection obvs. It was like deeper than that. They actually handed out plastic mirrors, like them ones you get in the hairdressers when they show you the back of your hair, and it was so weird. I think in general people think they look much worse than they actually fucking do. They like obsess about stuff like their hair or their eyebrows and there's like nothing wrong with their fucking hair or their fucking eyebrows, but they can barely go out of the fucking house. It's mental. Frankly the Belinda woman shouldn't have even brought up the moustache thing in the first place, because once you'd seen it you couldn't take your fucking eyes off it. And the woman, Lucy (Lucy with the long red hair not the short blond hair), she said that when she looked in the mirror she saw an afraid person. She said that she is afraid of everything. She said that she washes her hands over seventy times a day. She said that she can't go to the dentist in case the dentist has got germs on his gloves or on his pointer thing that he puts in your teeth. She said that if a murderer was running towards her with a knife her first reaction wouldn't be 'Don't stab me!', it would be 'Where was that knife last because I bet it's not clean.' I had to start coughing at that point. People are so fucking weird. Lucy said did we think she was weird, and we all shook our heads. And then Fleur said, actually, it was a bit weird but at least Lucy knew it was weird and isn't that usually half the problem? And we all laughed and agreed that it was, perhaps, a bit weird but, you know, don't worry about it. And then she felt better, which, let's face it, is weird too. Anyway, it was fun. Fleur said that by the end of the course we would be the 'mistresses of our own destiny'. I said to Sarah on the way home that I doubted that for Lucy. She was afraid of her own shadow. And that Belinda would be more of a master with *that* moustache. Sarah said she thought she'd like to go again next week and I said I would too. I sort of felt taller, you know? Not actually literally taller. Oh, I don't know. That sounds totally fucking lame.

Anyway, the day after Sarah got mugged, my mum said the community centre was all roped off so no free lunches for the homeless, and no mirrors for afraid people. And the road would be closed all day and the park too. And it was. There were lines of policemen in fluorescent tops walking all over the grass looking for something. My mum said she didn't know what they were looking for but, whatever it was, it would be evidence.

I told her about the drug smuggler in the corner and my mum said she shouldn't have been allowed out of prison, not for anything. And I said that if Billy OD'd she'd insist on being at the hospital, whatever. And she said that was an utterly ridiculous point to make because she was not a drug smuggler and Billy was not going to OD.

As soon as we got home I switched on the TV and basically I've done fuck all, all day, except watch crime bulletins. My mum rang Mrs Backhouse who said I should take as long as I like – which probably means she's just glad to get her class sizes down for a bit. I pretended to read my course book but FML what's *Jane Eyre* when you have got an actual drama on your fucking doorstep. A 'drama unfolding' they said on the TV. I keep forgetting that Sarah isn't here and keep looking out the window for her car. And every time the phone rings I jump right out of my skin. What if she dies? What if she fucking dies? What am I gonna do then?

9

Sarah

Day One – 10 p.m.

Sometimes it's dark and silent. Totally silent. That's when I've dis-appeared completely. That's when I start to dream. And, honestly, the dreaming is better than the darkness, until I wake up. And then it's dark again until suddenly the sound snaps on again. And I can hear everything around me.

It must be late. The sounds from the ward that I'd got used to during the day have gone. I don't think anyone is here. There's no rustling or quiet chatting. Just the hums and beeps and wheezes of the machines that are keeping me alive.

I can't have been here more than a day or so. I'm trying to piece it all together but sometimes my dreams are getting confused with the reality. I know I'm in hospital. I think I'm in a coma. I think that if I try really hard, I should be able to get my brain working again. I know I've got to try to communicate but if no one is watching me, no one is trying to find out if I'm still in here, how are they going to know?

And then I hear a sigh. Very close to my ear. And the sound of fabric on fabric as if someone is uncrossing and crossing their legs. And a foot squeaking across the floor. And then another sigh. Then the tapping begins.

Tap, tap-tap, tap. Tap, tap-tap, tap.

It's slow. It sounds like plastic on metal.

Tap, tap-tap, tap. Tap, tap-tap, tap.

I don't know why I suddenly feel afraid, but I do. I'm trying to understand. I've been mugged. I had a husband. A husband. He is now dead. He was killed. Maybe he was murdered. Maybe they were trying to murder me too. They've certainly done a pretty good job.

Tap, tap-tap, tap.

I hear the door shoot open.

'Excuse me!'

It's a startled woman's voice. She sounds nervous.

'What?'

A man's voice. Angry. Arrogant.

'You're not supposed to be here! Who are you?'

There are footsteps.

'I'm sorry but you have to leave.'

'What do you mean, I have to leave?'

'Who are you?'

'I met you yesterday, remember? I'm the brother.'

'The brother? Oh, you. It's you. Well ...'

'I didn't leave my number. I thought I'd just pop back, when it was quieter, you know. Look, I don't want to get in the way. I know how hard you ladies have to work. All hours. Look at you. You must be exhausted.'

The brother. Sounds like a smooth talker.

'Well, that's OK. Thank you. I'm sure it will be OK.'

It's the one who wears the leggings.

'It's just you have to sign in and stuff. You know, security. We can't have just anyone pitching up, can we? Plus you probably know the husband has died. So, could be a murder enquiry. The police will be all over us.'

'I did hear about Adam. Poor chap. Good bloke.'

'But we mustn't talk about that in here. In case she hears. You know.'

'What, you mean she's still in there? I thought they said she was brain dead.'

'Shhh. Come outside, please. We mustn't upset the patient – just in case she can hear. Some coma victims are locked in, you see. They can hear but they can't communicate. A living hell really. Come through and I'll explain.'

'You know what? I'm gonna split. I've got stuff to do. But I will come back. Promise. Are you on tomorrow night? Look after my girl for me, won't you.'

Their voices are trailing off down the corridor. Planning to meet the next night. Lisa's on the same shift. He'll come by after work. He's a businessman, he says. I wonder what he does. Sounds like a fob-off. Then his voice is nearer again.

'... just forgot my wallet ... yes, sure ... see you tomorrow ... yeah ...' he's shouting down the corridor.

He is walking back towards me.

He has a sing-song voice. Breathy and low. Weirdly frightening. He's whispering but he's close to me. It's so loud and so close it fills my brain. It fills the dark with dread. I am alone and afraid.

'Bye, Saaaaraaaah. Seeee youuuu tommmmmooooorrrooow.'

The door clicks shut.

Is he trying to kill me?

10

Kelly

Day One – 10.30 p.m.

The late-night bulletin has no more information than the earlier ones. No one is saying anything. Some twat of a policeman is going on about how crime is lower in the area than it's ever been, which is fucking LOL. People just don't report anything any more cos they know the police are like shite.

My mum got a call from them just before we had tea. She had her special telephone voice on. They are coming tomorrow at four. They are conducting investigations. Door-to-fucking-door. Blah-di-fucking-blah.

My mum comes in my room and says it's time for bed. And because I must look like shit she says that it must've been like a random mugging so stop worrying, and Sarah is gonna be fine, and why don't I clear the fucking floor up once in a while. She climbs over the piles of clothes and magazines and sits on my bed like she did before Billy got so needy. She says that they were just in the wrong place at the wrong time. That no one would want to harm yuppies. I can think of quite a few people who would have liked to hurt Adam, actually. Adam is Sarah's husband. Did I tell you that? In fact no one really liked Adam at all. He was a total tosser. I didn't say that to my mum. Obvs. She's Catholic. And she always says you shouldn't speak ill of the dead. And she says, 'Where were you anyway, Kelly? Last night', like really serious. And I say, 'I was at Sarah's, Mum. Like every Thursday.' And she says, 'But she wasn't in. She was out with Adam.' And I say, 'Yeah, I was doing my coursework on her dining-room table as usual until Adam came home, and I was so into it that I thought I may as well finish.' And she says, 'But you were late, right? What time did you come in?' And I say, 'Fuck my life, Mum, I don't know. About ten? Don't you want me to do my homework or something? Do you want me to fail all my exams?' And she says, 'It was later.' And I say, 'What are you trying to say, Mum, that I mugged Sarah? That I killed Adam? Yeah, that's it, Mum. I totally did it.' And then she gets really cross and she leaves. And she says, 'Just shut up, Kelly. Shut up. Stop talking while I think.' She was definitely crying.

11

Sarah

Day Two – 6 a.m.

'Morning, Sarah. And how are you today? You're in hospital. Time to wake up. It's raining but we expect a bit of rain in the spring, right? Better than snow!'

I can hear. I can hear. The beeping sound is back. The click, click, click, click is back. The tapping has gone. The man has gone. Who was that man? My brother. Who the fuck am I?

'Time to wake up now, Sarah. My name's Beth. You're in HOSPITAL.'

Morning, Beth. Nice to hear you.

'Are Mum and Dad in yet?'

The other nurse. Lucinda. The Irish one.

'They're getting tea. I've never known two people drink so much tea.'

'It's not the dad.'

I love my dad.

'What did the police say yesterday? My shift ended just after they arrived.'

'Well...'

Beth lowers her voice, but not so I can't hear. They're funny. They tell EVERYBODY *not to talk about stuff in front of me, then do it themselves.*

'Adam, the husband, has had his PM.'

What's a PM?

'He was killed by a blow to the head.'

Killed? KILLED?

'What, he hit the pavement too then, like her?'

'No, that's what's odd. His was a direct-impact injury. That's what Briggsy said. You know Briggsy on the lower ground floor?'

'Maybe they were after him all the time and Sarah was just an innocent bystander.'

'Yeah, I can't imagine anyone would randomly mug someone who was six foot four, would they? I mean, you'd have to really plan how to take down someone who was that big, right? There can't be many muggers daft enough to see a six-foot-four guy walking along and think, ooh, I must mug him. You'd have to be crazy. You wouldn't get a second chance. Not unless you were a really good shot. He was massive.'

Six foot four? 'If he's six foot four and he got a massive head trauma, wouldn't the murderer have to be like really, really tall?'

They are both giggling.

'Calling all units,' – *in a police radio voice* – 'please be on the lookout for the jolly green giant in a balaclava.'

'Or a mugger on stilts.'

'Or Bruce Lee giving a flying kick? Hang on, though, maybe he was attacked when he was already on the pavement?'

'No. That's what I said, but Briggsy said he must have been standing up. He said they can tell by the blood-spatter distribution. But you know what that lot are like. They change their minds all the time. And then there's all the stuff they don't tell you.'

I can't picture anyone called Adam.

'Have they released the body?'

'God, no. It'll be ages. It's a murder investigation now.'

'Have they got any suspects?'

'No, but they should have CCTV of the street. There's a traffic camera on that bit of road cos it's right by a park and near a school.'

'So they'll find him.'

'Him or them.'

'What, a gang?'

Someone arrives.

'Probably. Ah, Mrs Beresford! Got your tea?'

'Yes, thank you, Beth. How's Sarah?'

'We'll be back in about ten minutes to take her for a brain scan. Now don't forget to do the talking, Mum. We'd like to see some movement today. Her meds are right down. Mr Malin is around later and he's going to be asking about progress.'

Progress. What progress? I can't move anything. I'm stuck in this dead body. I can't get out.

'The physio is coming this afternoon, too. We need to get those legs moving or we'll be getting bedsores.'

'She was such a pretty little girl. Brian, wasn't she a pretty little girl?'

'She was always a lovely girl, June. She still is.'

My dad.

There's a loud noise. Really loud. Like a foghorn on a boat. It's very close. Maybe I'm dreaming. There are really loud crashes. No voices. I want to get away.

I want to shut out the noise.

I don't want to be here.

Who was that man in my room?

What does he want from me?

What will happen when he comes back?

12

Kelly

Day Two – 11 a.m.

The police are coming at four. It's Saturday. No school. Sarah's face has been all over the telly all morning. There's pictures of Adam too. A picture of their wedding when Sarah doesn't even look like Sarah. She was so glamorous. She wore a lace silk dress with a long bit at the back that stuck out. Like a model or a film star or something. There's more pictures of Sarah than there are of Adam. And they're saying that they got mugged. But they say that it must've been planned. That it wasn't random. They don't say how they know. Pigs never give much away.

Mum has taken Billy to football. The police are actually here already – next door in Sarah's house. They've put tape outside the front gate that says POLICE on it in blue letters. It doesn't seem right that they should be going through all her stuff. If I stand in our hall I can hear what they are saying. I can even hear their radios. They keep going up and down the stairs.

Anna from down the road is already here. My mum's invited her for coffee and she's not even in. Billy's probably got her to stay and watch. He's so fucking pathetic. 'Watch me score a goal, Mum. Watch me, watch me', and then he won't even tackle anyone. One game last year he never even touched the fucking ball the entire game. I'm not even lying. He just stands there with his hands on his hips, pointing occasionally. His coach calls him pretty boy. Says he won't tackle cos he don't wanna get any mud on his pretty little face.

Anna says the police are going to her house at three. She used to do cleaning and ironing and stuff at Sarah's. She only liked doing it when Sarah was home. Said it was creepy when it was just Adam in the house. See – I told you no one liked Adam.

Adam hated Anna too. Obvs things went like gross bad when Adam said that Anna's son had nicked his car. Did I tell you about the car getting nicked? OK, so the car got nicked just after they moved in, so like no one knew them that well yet. All they knew was that they were yuppies. My mum had told everyone, right. So obvs everyone wanted to know what yuppies looked like. So every time anyone went by their house, they'd be like looking through the window to see what they could see. On this one particular day, Adam had left his set of keys in the front door, when he'd come back from the offy and someone took the keys out of the front door and drove off in his car. Their car. Just like that. I mean it sort of serves him right, don't you think? You can't just leave your fucking keys in your front door and expect people not to take them, right? Not in South Tottenham you can't. Twat. Anyway, Adam ran after the car all the way down our road to the junction with White Hart Lane. Bet Nathan wasn't expecting that. Turns out that Adam can run really fast. Like seriously fast. And he was shouting and swearing at Nathan but Nathan just managed to stay ahead of him and not get seen or nothing. Nathan must've nearly shat himself. LOL. It *was* Nathan by the way. Anna never admitted it. Mum said Anna just told Nathan to bring it back like right now. Which he did. No harm done, right? He just parked it up the end of the road that night and chucked the keys by the doorstep. Getting back your stolen car, around here, is like total respect, right? So I don't know what Adam was so pissed for. The thing was that even though Adam got the car back, Adam had a feeling it was Nathan that did it and he knew that Anna knew that Adam knew that Nathan did it. OMG, this is confusing. So every time Adam saw Anna he'd be like, 'How's Nathan then, Anna?' And Anna had a go at Nathan again. And then Nathan got really pissed with Adam and tells all his mates that Adam is a tosser. So that's why no one likes Adam. Well, one of the reasons.

Anyway, Anna is here and she's making the coffee herself cos she knows where everything is cos she's here half her life cos her daughter-in-law hates her. 'The police think Adam got murdered,' I say to Anna. And she goes, 'Well, he got what he deserved, right?' but with like a thick Greek accent. So I say, 'You wanna watch it, Anna, cos they might think it's Nathan, you know?' And she starts swearing in Greek. And I say, 'But, you know, there are loads of people who would wanna do some serious damage to Adam.' And she stops swearing and looks at me. 'Like who?' she goes. So I say what about that Iranian guy from Finchley who kept coming around asking for money and didn't she see him sometimes standing over the road like waiting for Adam cos like Adam owed him a thousand or something and he told Adam he was gonna do his kneecaps. Sarah told me about it. Anna says she thinks she remembers him. And did I say Iranian? Says she thinks she had seen someone standing in the bushes opposite their house. And there is that Cypriot bloke in the TV place on Green Lanes who said Adam had like borrowed a TV off him and never paid. He said that unless Adam got the money he would, like, have an accident. That's how Sarah put it. An accident! She was so worried they were gonna like pour petrol through the letterbox or something like they did with them people in Hackney. She probably paid that one back too. She was always paying people back. We were at the newsagent one day, me and her, and the Indian lady behind the counter was like, 'You should be ashamed of your husband.' To Sarah. And she was like, 'What?' And the Indian lady said that Adam came in every day and got cigarettes and stuff and would never pay. He would always say he would pay tomorrow. She said he was a bully to her husband and that she wanted to hit him with a stick. (Actually that bit was quite funny.) Anyhow the bill was like £200. She paid that too. Anna is shaking her head. 'You're right,' she says. 'There are loads of people who would wanna do some serious damage to Adam,' except she says it in her weird Greek accent.

My mum gets back just as she's saying that. 'Jesus, Mary and Joseph, Anna. What are you saying? They were mugged!' she says. 'For their credit cards, I'll bet you. They'll have taken all their jewellery and wallets and all. You see.'

So while Anna goes off to be interviewed at her house, my mum makes herself a cup of tea and waits for her turn. And I'm still standing in the hall with my head against the wallpaper.

13

Sarah

Day Two – 12 noon

The sound comes back on, the room seems full of people. Someone turns a tap on and water runs. I imagine a glass of water. Cold water with ice cubes. Or a tall glass of Coke with a slice of lemon in it, with condensation running down the sides. I wonder if I'll ever have a drink again. The tap squeaks off. The door handle snaps open and I hear feet shuffling and chairs scraping.

'Mr and Mrs, um, Beresford. You know why we are all here. We don't usually conduct this type of meeting here but the Detective Inspector wants Mr Malin to update him on your daughter's progress. Perhaps we could retire to the family room as soon as possible so that we don't disturb Sarah any more than we have to. Do you understand, Detective Inspector Langlands?'

That was a lady's voice. She sounds like a caring woman. Someone who genuinely wants to help. I can imagine my dad nodding and rubbing his chin. There is a small cough and clearing of a throat.

'Mr and Mrs Beresford.'

Oh lord, this man has the most annoying voice.

'Once again please accept our sincere sympathies on behalf of the force at this very difficult time. As you both know, we are now conducting a murder investigation. Although this is a very difficult time for you we do need to ask you a few questions concerning your daughter and her, um, husband.'

He sounds like an officious twit.

'This is nothing to worry about, June, Brian.'

The softly spoken woman again.

'As you know, as your victim support liaison I can talk you through anything you don't fully understand when Detective Inspector Langlands has asked you more questions. We just need to make sure all our paperwork is in order before we can go any further with the investigation. If you have any concerns we can talk later.'

Honestly. What the fuck. Go on, Dad. Tell them to get out. Tell them I'm in a coma and we should be concentrating on making me better. Why does it feel like no one is actually trying to help me? Where are the doctors?

'No, no. You go ahead with your questions.'

That's my mother.

'We did already speak to one of your colleagues yesterday …'

Thanks, Dad.

'I'm well aware of that, Mr Beresford. I'm afraid that we are now treating this as a murder investigation. We don't believe it was simply a mugging. We think that the couple were targeted. That means we will need to ask you some further questions – this is just the start. So, do you know what your daughter and son-in-law were doing in White Hart Lane on the night in question? It was ten o'clock at night in a not very pleasant area.'

'It's an up-and-coming area, Tottenham. Sarah always said there are some very nice bits, didn't she, Brian?'

'She was worried at first.'

'She said she thought that there were gangs of kids that were very rough. One-parent families, you know. Not much discipline. We were a bit worried when they first moved there but the neighbours are … well, they're not really *our* sort but Sarah said they were nice. Good people. There was a Brenda. I believe she was next door. She had a daughter. And the Greek lady down the road did a bit of ironing for Sarah. Have you spoken to them? They'll tell you what a lovely girl Sarah was. How she wasn't one to get into fights.'

'We are due to take statements from the neighbours.'

The policeman chap sounds like he has a short fuse.

'What we're unsure of, Mrs Beresford – sorry to interrupt – but what do you think they were doing there so late?'

'Is ten o'clock late? I don't think the youth of today would call that late. Brian and I often don't go to bed until ten thirty, do we, Brian?'

'I don't think we know, do we, June?'

That's my dad.

'When was the last time you spoke to your daughter, Mrs Beresford?'

I'm sorry but that sounds very accusatory to me. Like I wouldn't be in a coma if I had phoned my parents more often.

'She called me that day, didn't she, Brian? She calls me every day but she didn't mention they were going out.'

'She calls you every day? Isn't that quite unusual for a young woman to contact her parents every day?'

Oh, make your mind up. One minute you complain it's not enough contact, next minute it's too much.

'No, not really. Sarah always calls. She's always on the phone. Always wants to know all about what we were doing. You know.'

'OK. Right.'

He's losing patience.

'So destination not known … Hmm. So, can I ask, and this may sound personal but it's not meant to … to your knowledge, was your daughter happy in her marriage?'

Was I?

'Well, of course she was happy. They had a newly done-up house, not in a terribly good area admittedly, but it was very nicely done inside. And she had a new job – a good job. At a publishing house. Hall & Brown Books.'

Hall & Brown?

'They sent some beautiful flowers today, didn't they, Brian? But you aren't allowed flowers in hospital now. They have germs, the nurse said. So they put the flowers in the nurses' station. Sarah won't mind. She'll be pleased that the nurses had something nice. She never complains, does our Sarah. I think they were, weren't they, Brian?'

'Yes, June. Sorry. What about? Are we still on the flowers?'

'No, Brian. About them being happy.'

'Oh yes. She probably was.'

'Probably, Mr Beresford?'

'Yes, very probably. She was quiet. A quiet girl.'

He doesn't sound sure.

'Is there anything else, Inspector? I'm sure Mr and Mrs Beresford have answered enough questions.'

'Nope, that's it really. Thank you both. Dr Malin?'

There's a snap of a book closing.

'Yes, so why don't you, Mr and Mrs Beresford, go and get some tea, both of you, while I cover the medical side of things.'

'Thank you, doctor.'

The door opens and closes.

'I have a few questions for you, though, Dr Malin, if you don't mind?'

'Go ahead then, I have ward rounds in ten.'

The voices become quieter.

'What's the prognosis then, Dr Malin?'

'It's Mr Malin. Not Doctor. Mister. We don't yet know. We did an MRI this morning but it wasn't conclusive. There's too much swelling and it's too early to tell, really. We don't know if there is any brain activity at all. But we hope there is. If we're lucky, we would expect to see some progress within three days of the trauma taking place. In my experience we will pretty much know for sure what is going on within ten days. If we aren't making any progress by that time then we will have to look at other things. There are only so many tests we can do.'

What does that mean? I've lost track of time. How long have I been here?

'Also, doctor, FYI. I'm putting some extra security on the ward.'

'It's Mr. Not Dr. Can you get that written down in your goddam little book, man? Security? What on earth for? It's hard enough to get in here as it is. There is absolutely no reason for you starting to pollute my wards with your ...'

They've gone.

This is me thinking.

That is all I can do.

I have just remembered something about my mother. I think it's a memory but it could be a dream. A bad dream. I was trying to tell her something and she wouldn't listen. She was busy in the kitchen and I was hiding between the folds of her skirt. Flecks of washing-up bubbles kept splashing down my T-shirt. I was hold-ing on tight to her warm leg through the cold crisp cotton skirt but she kept trying to move away. She said, 'Sarah, will you stop it!' but I didn't let go. She picked me up with her hot, wet hands and put me on a stool by the draining board. She dried her hands on her apron and sighed and asked me what on earth was the mat-ter and why couldn't I just let her get on with the meal and that Dad was going to be home any minute now and he'd be cross if the meal wasn't ready and he didn't like casserole at the best of times. She wiped my face with the tea towel. It smelt of cake mix and old gravy. And I pointed to the garden. Pointed at the man in the garden. And she turned and looked at him and then suddenly threw down the tea towel and slapped me hard across the cheek. Slapped me so hard that I slipped sideways off the stool and landed heavily onto the floor, my legs tangled up. 'Don't start with your lies, Sarah,' she shouted. 'You're nothing but a little liar', and she went back to the sink. 'Mr Eades is just a nice old man. Everyone round here thinks the world of him. We all do our bit for Care in the Community. And pottering around in our shed is doing you NO HARM, MISSY. Mrs Garland at the end of the road has him do her lawns. He does everyone's windows. How would it look? HOW WOULD IT LOOK, SARAH, IF YOU START MAKING UP LIES ABOUT HIM? You will bring shame to this family. Shame and scandal. You don't begin to understand, you selfish little fool. You think you can open up those big blue eyes of yours and get away with lying,' she said, as I picked myself up from the floor. 'Don't you go talking to your father either,' she said in a low, quiet voice. A threatening voice. And the man in the garden walked past the window. And he nodded at my mother and tipped his hat. And she smiled a thin-lipped smile and said, 'Bye, Mr Eades, thanks again.' Her cheeks were hot as she looked over at me on the floor. I stopped crying. I can't remember any more.

When I stopped dreaming I couldn't hear anything.

I have sunk deeper.

14

Kelly

Day Two – 3.30 p.m.

At half past three the police arrive. Early. There are two police-men, one in a uniform who doesn't say anything much and needn't have bothered coming if you ask me, and this detective bloke called Langlands. I've seen Langlands before. He was on TV yesterday and he once came and gave a twattish talk in assembly the day after the languages block got burnt down, about how not to play with matches or leave cigarette tabs burning. He interviewed a load of kids including Kathryn Cowell and Wino, but mostly Year 13, who all smoked. The fire-men hadn't found the petrol can by that point. The police still thought the fire was an accident. We all knew, though. And we all stood there taking this crap about smouldering tabs turning into configurations or something. I think that was the word. It don't sound right now.

Langlands talks down to people and he thinks that nobody notices. He thinks he comes across as being nice. But he's just a twat. My mum is so onto him it's hilarious – even if she is old. It's his, like, default mode to be totally patronising. He also fancies himself as a bit of a like secret agent. Jason Bourne or 007. They brought along that victim support lady with them too, Gill Brannon, who my mum will definitely say is totally tea and tampons. That's her favourite phrase. Like a school nurse or one of those politicians who wants you to sign something, you know. Busybodies, my mum calls them. Drippy. She shakes my mum's hand and rubs her arm – my mum's arm I mean – and says that while she is primarily looking after Sarah's interests, there are often 'many victims in a crime' and that if she feels that she would like some 'counselling or advice' she should 'get in contact'. During which Langlands yawns and sits himself down. Then she presses another one of her little fliers into my mum's hand. She must get through a lot of photocopying. So, anyhow, they're all here and sat in the front room that only gets used when there's like royalty in the house. It smells of damp dog in there even though we don't have one. I'd quite like a dog but not really if it ends up smelling like that.

So, anyway, my mum talks in her posh voice and offers everyone tea. And I'm standing in the hall with my hands behind my back leaning against the radiator. Just so you can really picture the scene, I have my school uniform on. Question: why would I be wearing my uniform on a Saturday? My mum asked me the exact same thing when I just came down the stairs. And I answered, 'My jeans are in the wash. I spilt soup on them.'

Which isn't true. And besides I do have plenty of other stuff. I just thought to myself that for such an official occasion I should look like what I am – you know, like a schoolchild. Fuck my life, Sarah would be proud of me. My mum had been about to start an argument with me about it, when the pigs had rung the doorbell.

'While I make some tea, would you like to talk to my daughter Kelly at all, Mr Langlands?' says my mum, as she sweeps out of the room like the fucking Queen or something. 'Detective Inspector,' says the Detective Inspector. D'ya see? Told you he was a twat. He's looking at me. And I am holding my breath. And my cheeks go pink. And I stare down at my feet in my Lisa Simpson slippers that I got from Father Christmas.

And the tea-and-tampons lady goes 'Detective Inspector,' and she touches him on his arm. I bet there is like a social worker handbook that they give you and on page 1 it says rub someone's arm to make them feel liked or something. BTW Langlands obvs thinks she is totally fucking mental. He is looking at his sleeve like it's got shit on it. And she goes, very quietly so I can only just hear her, 'Kelly is fourteen, Detective Inspector. She's a schoolgirl. She was not close to Sarah. Sarah was quite obviously friends with Mrs McCarthy.'

My mum comes back with a plate of digestives. She goes to each person in turn with the plate to buy time while the tea settles (that's the word my mum uses), and they politely decline apart from the silent policeman who takes one then gets a look from Langlands as if to say, what the fuck are you doing eating a fucking digestive, you fucking cock? My mum staggers back in again with the tray. Langlands is going through his notes. Tea and tampons is carefully writing a list with a purple ink pen in one of those cheap spiral-bound pads you get at Sainsbury's. And the other policeman is munching through his digestive as quickly as he can and with some difficulty, looks like. It is actually really hard to eat a digestive if you don't have a drink to have with it. I always have mine with my Ribena.

'Mrs McCarthy. I'd just like to speak with you, thank you,' says Langlands. 'I'm sure your daughter here has far more fascinating things to be doing.' Cock. My mum kind of nods her head towards the stairs, which obvs I ignore and carry on standing by the open door, against the radiator in the hall.

'Mrs McCarthy, first of all can I establish how long you have been living at this address?' My mum coughs a little cough and then launches into the entire fucking McCarthy ancestry – all the way back to Ireland and the fucking potato famine. Can't tell you how many times I've had to suffer listening to that one. Great Uncle Alan and Great Auntie Orlagh. And Grandad Alfred and Grandma Mabel. My mum obvs catches that look on my face that says WTF. And she goes, 'Jesus, Mary and Joseph, Kelly Louise Jane McCarthy', which is a lot of names for one sentence. 'Would you kindly go to your room, right this second.' So I go up the stairs and the door gets closed between the sitting room and the hallway so from the stairs all I can hear is like a murmur of conversation. My mum is doing most of the talking, lapsing in and out of her fucking Queen Mother voice every so often.

So eventually there's a rattle of cups and saucers and the door opens and out comes the silent policeman and Mrs Brannon followed by my mum and Langlands. Langlands now has a digestive too. And he says, 'And you can't corroborate that there were any financial problems – any outstanding debts that the couple were concerned about at all?' And my mum says that, yes, she had heard about the Cypriot TV guy in Green Lanes and the Iranian guy from Finchley and she says, yes, there was trouble with the Indian newsagent. But says she didn't realise that all that stuff was anything more than hearsay. Gossip. She says she knows the Indian lady from the corner shop and that there is quite often a nasty-looking chap over the road waiting for Adam. She says, 'But isn't this just a case of being in the wrong place at the wrong time', like she's the fucking detective!

I'm standing on the bottom step of the stairs, holding onto the bannisters and sliding in my socks over the lip of the stair and plopping onto the floor. Then climbing back onto the step and doing it again. Clare used to say it's good for your calf muscles. Anyway, my mum has the front door open and they are filing out and Langlands peers back at me over his notebook.

'Have I met you before, Kelly?' he says.

'Nah, I don't think so,' I say, hopping back up a step and sliding off again.

And he goes, 'You're at South Haringey Secondary, are you?'

And I go, 'Yeah', but politely, you know, obvs. Not just like, 'YEAH' in a rude way.

And he goes, 'Perhaps I met you there after the arson attack?'

And I go, 'I don't think so, Detective um Langlands. What's arson mean?'

And he didn't even reply. He just went off with his fucking digestive. Cock.

15

Sarah

Day Two – 6 p.m.

I've been awake for ages – if I can call it awake. I mean conscious in my own head ... Anyway, for ages it has been silent. Not the usual sound of the ward and the nurses. Dying from the outside in. Then just now the volume came on again. I can hear the familiar hum of the life-support machine and a new clicking sound. Above the heaving of the respirator and the buzzing and the beeping. A gentle but repetitive clicking. Sometimes I am here and sometimes I'm not.

'Brian? Brian. What are you doing?'

'June, I'm reading the paper. What does it look like I'm doing?'

'They said to talk to her, Brian.'

'I thought you were going to talk to her.'

'I'm too busy worrying, Brian. What do you think we should do about Adam?'

'Adam?'

'Adam!'

'What do you mean what should we do about Adam? We can't do much for Adam now. He's dead.'

'I mean about Sarah and Adam. Shouldn't we go and sort out the house or something. Someone's got to go and sort out all the bills and things, haven't they?'

She pauses and the clicking continues. I think she is knitting. Knitting sounds about right.

'I mean, has he left a will? Or does it all just go to Sarah because she's his wife, or not?'

'If they had a will, they will have left everything to each other, I expect. And if they haven't, it all goes to her anyway.'

'What if ... you know?'

'Then usually it goes to the parents, I think. Unless they have a dog home in mind. Some people don't have the sense they were born with.'

'Carol has spoken to Adam's parents. They wanted to come to visit but they've gone back to Cheshire. Trouble with work. The police are taking care of all that, June. The bank will let us know if the cards are used. That Gill lady said not to worry. Let's just focus on getting Sarah back. As far as a will goes, I think it always automatically goes to the wife.'

'It'll all be debt. That's what it'll be.'

'We don't know that, June.'

'He should never have smoked.'

'I don't suppose that made much of a difference in the end, did it, June?'

There's a pause. The knitting needles click.

'I shall pray about it.'

'Why don't you do that back at the Travelodge, dear?'

I don't think there can be a God. There isn't one in here. It's so dark, so completely fucking dark and I'm alone. I can only imagine putting my arms out in front of me, searching for something to make sense of my world. It's like I'm suspended in nothing. Voices echo through the darkness. Sometimes I can hear them perfectly and sometimes I can hear a bit and sometimes, when it's worst of all, it is just silent. The voices seem to come from somewhere way above me. I'm an ant stuck in a big empty bucket. No, smaller than that. I am plankton stuck at the bottom of a deep lagoon. I have no idea which way is out.

So I need to make a channel in my brain from A to B. That's what the doctor said. But how am I supposed to do that? They didn't say how. It's fine for them to say to do it, but they didn't say how.

And Adam? I can't remember Adam.

Beth and Lucinda are here.

'Are they running on time?'

'He's doing the rounds with the students.'

'God, we'll be here all day. Have you done the chart?'

'All done.'

'The swelling is really improving.'

'She's pretty underneath.'

'You wouldn't have said that on Friday morning.'

'Have you seen that wedding picture that was on the telly? She's not normal for Tottenham.'

'Why would anyone do that to her?'

'It's Tottenham. You know what it's like up there. It's a jungle. My gran used to have a friend in Tottenham. Turned out she was actually living next door to a crack den.'

'What, your gran lived next to a crack den?'

'No, my gran's friend. She'd lived there all her life, right, and one day she decided to get a man round to cut down her hedge cos since her husband had died no one had done it for ages and by accident the bloke cut down the hedge at the side as well as at the front and the bloke from next door, he was African or something, he comes round and has a right go at her cos his front door was in full view and how was he supposed to run his business? How was she supposed to know? It's not something you usually consider before you trim your privet.'

'Did she move?'

'I don't know. My gran died. She was old, though. Tottenham's just a multicultural soup, isn't it? That's what they say. The Greeks hate the Cypriots. The Iranians hate the Iraqis. The Irish hate everyone. Actually everyone hates everyone.'

'Here comes Malin.'

There's a cough.

'Right now, gather round now. Uh huh. Good. Now we have here a patient, Sarah Beresford' – *yes, that's me* – 'who is in a comatose state after a head trauma, which we believe has caused an intra-axial haemorrhage.'

Why can't he explain what it means?!

'Nurse, are the meds up to date? Good, uh huh. As you can see, she has also suffered severe bruising about the face but has, in fact, no other significant injuries.'

Bruising to the face, eh? Lovely.

'These bruises along the lateral cheek and this swelling around the eyes, these are not the result of direct impact. These are ruptured blood vessels caused by a blow to the back of the skull that resulted in a compound fracture. We got inconclusive results from the last MRI. When is the next MRI scheduled for? Uh huh. Good. Does anyone have any questions? Yes?'

I have a question. When am I going to wake up?

'The blow to the back of the head, yes. Good point! The police believe the trauma was caused by impact with the pavement. It appears the victim, um, yes, Sarah' – *he forgets names quickly* – 'was probably pushed from the front and hit her head upon contact with the ground. There are no other injuries, either on the hands, as we might expect from fending off an attack, or from breaking her fall or, indeed, from the initial push. It appears the push must have been very fast indeed and caught her off balance. This is consistent with the initial police report that suggests a hit-and-run-style mugging. Maybe the muggers approached on bikes – this is more and more prevalent in socially neglected parts of London. It's silent and quick, and cheap to get a bike. Or perhaps the attackers were hidden in bushes. The entrance to the park is very close to the crime scene.'

I was off balance. I was pushed from the front. I hit my head on the pavement. Who pushed me? Why would someone hurt me? I didn't hurt anyone, did I? I don't hurt people. That much I know. Did my brother have anything to do with it?

Someone – one of the students I guess – is asking a question and I can't quite hear.

'That is a matter for the police not the medical profession. The facts of the crime are only necessary if required to assist with diagnosis or treatment. We are here to make people better, not to be detectives. Medicine, Mr Pickard. Stick to medicine.'

People are mumbling and shuffling and suddenly the only sound is the echoing beep and the heave of the respirator. Funny how everyone is happy to explain how I got in here but no one will tell me how to get out. The door clicks open.

'Has he gone? What'd he say?'

Beth and I guess Lucinda are back.

'Only that she was pushed over. We knew that, didn't we? Must have pushed her pretty damn hard. Are Mum and Dad here or have they gone?'

'They're with victim liaison at the Travelodge. Something about the missing credit cards.'

I wonder what else was stolen. I wonder if they took my house keys. I wonder if I have house keys. I wonder if I have a house.

16

Kelly

Day Two – 7 p.m.

Usually when I'm up to my ears in shit, I text Clare. This is not your average amount of up-to-my-ears-in-shit, though. This is mega. This is fucking swimming in shit.

I was thinking about Clare today, again. I do a lot after what happened. We had stopped being friends (not actually stopped being friends but, you know, not on the phone every ten fucking seconds), a long time before anything happened with her and Wino. And even though everyone said it wasn't my fault what happened with him, I will always think that it was. If I'd been with her nothing would have happened. I could have stopped him. Clare was never as mouthy as me.

Did I tell you that Clare's dad committed suicide? Not like recently. Like ages ago. Like when she was nine or something. My mum said Clare's dad was presupposed to suicide. I don't know what that means. Maybe that isn't the word. I think it means he was a bit of a schizo. And he was made that way. Mum says.

I sat next to him at dinner this one time, when I was over at Clare's. They always had a proper sit-down dinner – every night. My mum always says she wants us to do that. But since my dad left we just have it on our laps and watch episodes of *Come Dine With Me*. He was a scientist or something, Clare's dad. He looked like he was. Like super intelligent. You know, kind of small and with little round glasses that were all dirty and fuck knows how he saw out of them, and a goat beard. I told him I was learning the recorder, at school, you know, and he said that when I'd learned it I should look at taking up the bassoon. Who the fuck wants to play a fucking bassoon? Have you seen how fucking big they are? And anyone you ever see who plays a bassoon is a right fucking ponce – when they're playing it and when they're not playing it. You look like a ponce just carrying a bassoon. So I said, 'I'd rather play an oboe.' And he shook his head and said, 'Oboes are too penetrating. They get into your skull.' So I said, 'But bassoons are really fucking loud.' And he laughed and said if his daughter said a word like that, at nine, he would wash her mouth out with soap, lock her in a room and throw away the key. But he was still laughing when he said it. He committed suicide like three days later. I always slightly wondered if my thoughts on fucking bassoons had got anything to do with it.

When I first met Sarah, Clare got well funny with me. She was like, 'What d'ya wanna see her for. Who's she anyway? She's too old. She's too posh.' She got totally pissed at me when I changed my hair back from White Platinum too. I think she liked us being twins. She liked it when everybody stared at us. She even sat my French Speaking test for me one time. Like two summers ago. It was a supply teacher doing it. French supply teacher, even better. They don't check nothing. And since I hadn't done one fucking bit of revision, Clare just went in and did it for me. Just like fucking that. Genius. It was great having a twin. Sometimes it was. But Sarah said I should just try it out going brown. Said we could always dye it back. Said maybe Clare should change hers too. But she wouldn't.

It was around that time that she got funny about food. Clare, I mean. She was never up for going down McDonald's any more, and if we did she would just get a Diet Coke and sit behind it while the rest of us stuffed fries in our faces.

Then her fucking face went hairy. OMG. D'ya know what I mean? Like furry. I said to her, 'Your face has got fuzz all over it.' She said she had lost like three stone or something. Two stone maybe. So none of her fucking clothes fit no more. None of my fucking clothes fit her neither. I was like, 'Give them back to me if you're not even gonna fucking wear them.' She just said I was Little Miss Drama Queen of the Fucking Century.

Mum said since her dad died, she's just got away with murder. 'Can you imagine her dad letting her have hair that colour?' My mum said her mum spoilt her. I think her mum wasn't a scientist. I think she was a dinner lady. They were an odd match. That's what my mum said when Clare first went White Platinum. But cos she had White Platinum that meant I could have White Platinum too.

Obvs I know that is trashy, now. Obvs I know that in order to be invisible, you have to blend in. Then you won't get noticed. You won't get picked on. Then you disappear. I told Clare that. I told her to change her hair back. But she wouldn't. She should've. You don't get hurt if you're invisible.

17

Sarah

Day Two – 8 p.m.

I think it's Lucinda and Beth that are clanking around the room. They sound busy and stressed and tired.

'Wasn't Lisa down for tonight?'

Beth seems in a hurry.

'She's off sick. Something about period pains.'

Lucinda sounds young, younger than Beth anyway.

'Honestly! Period pains are for getting you out of hockey lessons at school. Literally, how bad can it be?'

'She said we should look out for Sarah's brother, though. He said he'd pop in again tonight.'

It's tonight already?

'Pop in?'

'Sarah's brother, yes.'

'Again?'

'OK, stop. Lisa said, "Sarah's brother is going to pop in again tonight." Am I not speaking English?'

'But he's not on the list. I checked earlier. That policeman was asking who had already been in to visit Sarah, and I told him only family. I looked on the list. He's not on the list.'

'Well, Beth, he should be. He is a family member. He is a BROTHER, right?'

Beth, don't leave me. Don't let him in. I don't like him.

'But how come he's been here twice and he's not been put on the list? And how come, both times, he came in when the rest of the family weren't here? Has anyone even mentioned a brother? We've heard about the sister. Carol. Did anyone actually ask the parents if they had a son? Jesus! What's his name anyway?'

The sound dies. I'm grateful.

Later, and I don't know how much later, I hear the tapping again. Tap tap-tap tap. Plastic on metal. Tap tap-tap tap. Tap tap-tap tap.

I don't even know if it's real.

But my fear is.

18

Kelly

Day Three – 10 a.m.

The nice nurse, the one called Beth, she said that Sarah would probably move today. Maybe wake up. Sunday, she said. Sunday would be a good day. She said that once Sarah was on less drug stuff her brain would start to work again. And she said she would call me. She even took my mobile number and said that if Sarah even so much as twitched or anything she would text me. I look at my phone just about every minute. I'm not even lying. I'm looking at it so much I have a pain in my wrist. I have RSJ – repetitive strain … injury. Can you get compensation for that?

I haven't even told you about the arson attack yet, have I? The one that Langlands was on about that took out the entire fucking languages block. But I can't tell you about that until I've told you about Kathryn Cowell and before I tell you about her, I have to tell you about my first day at South Haringey. This is before I even knew Sarah. I started in Year 7, when I was just eleven, at the beginning of September, and Sarah moved in like in the middle of September. It can't have been long after cos it was still really hot. She saw me on that day when I yanked Billy's arm. She saw me from her bedroom window upstairs that overlooks the bend in the road. She didn't see Wino on the other side of the road. She just saw me hurting Billy. But she never told my mum. She never said nothing about it until much later. She was good at saying nothing.

So it all started with this fucking locker key thing. It's my mum's fault. You see, everyone had to have their own padlock. It said so in the pack you get before you start at the school. You get given a locker, right, for all your stuff but it's up to you to lock it up otherwise all your stuff gets nicked. It doesn't say 'it may get nicked', it says 'it will get nicked'. That's what it's like at South Haringey Secondary. It's not a great area. There's like the Huntley Estate, that's one of them high rises, that's where Wino lives, then the Farringdon Estate, which is exactly the same but further up White Hart Lane. There's like two thousand kids at the school altogether.

So on my first day at South Haringey Secondary, each form was taken to the locker room and everyone was given a random number and you had to find your locker and put your padlock on it. My mum had got me this padlock from Halfords when she took Billy's bike in to get the seat fixed – he'd left it out the back again and the saddle had rusted and when his legs grew he couldn't move it up. Anyway, she got me this pink rubber padlock that is a bit fucking fancy as padlocks go. Most people just got a normal one but my mum thinks – and this is her fucking logic – that everyone is gonna have a plain padlock so better for me to have like a pink one that stands out so I can find my locker easier. There are numbers on the lockers. I told her that. She said how was she supposed to know. So I put all my stuff in my locker, my books for English and my coloured pencils, spare hairbands and stuff, and attached the fat rubber pink padlock and that was fine, right. Then at the end of the day I go back to the locker to pick up my bag. And I see the pink padlock and I put my key in, open it and ... well, FML, it wasn't my stuff. There was a half-bottle of vodka, and a brass lighter with a peace sign on and initials KOP in like pretend diamonds on it, and a pair of those boots that have like steel toe caps in (Sarah says they used to be called DMs) which were all dusty with dirty yellow laces, and then there was this metal thing that someone told me after was a knuckleduster. To start off with I thought all my stuff had been nicked. I'd hardly finished totally crapping myself when I felt someone grab my ponytail. I had a ponytail at that point – me and Clare had both started doing this really high ponytail thing. We looked like My Little fucking Pony. Anyway, I was fucking scared because he nearly snapped my goddam head off and I was being dragged backwards across the locker room. And this voice goes, 'What the fuck you doing in Kathryn's locker?' Actually he called her Kaffrin. They spoke like lame twats, all of them. So I was like, 'It's my locker. My stuff has gone.' I could hardly breathe. And he yanked me onto the ground and he said I'd better fucking keep out of his fucking way and out of Kaffrin's fucking locker and if he ever saw me or my stupid fucking ponytail again anywhere near her fucking locker he was gonna fucking do me, alright? I thought he might do me right there, but then a fight broke out at the other end of the locker room and Wino – that's who it was – just cleared off to watch, leaving me on the floor by the window.

I got up and stared at the locker again and after about five seconds I realised that the locker three along from the one that I had opened also had a fucking pink fucking rubber padlock. Kathryn Cowell had the exact same padlock as mine. I meant to go back to Halfords to ask them how they can fucking sell two fucking padlocks that take the same fucking key but I didn't. I mean how can they do that? Isn't that like illegal? I bought a new padlock on the way home and got in early the next day so I could swap it over. I got the same plain padlock like everyone else had, except Kathryn Cowell. It didn't matter, though, cos after that they knew who I was. You didn't want Wino to know who you were.

I didn't tell my mum. She wouldn't have been able to do anything or if she did she would have made it like totally worse. I didn't say anything to anyone. Until later, when I told Sarah. That's when we decided to dye my hair back to what it looks like now. I didn't really get what she was saying from the start. I get it now, though. It's easier to look plain. Can you see why it's like totally the right thing to do? If Sarah was here now she would say 'Don't draw attention to yourself, Kelly. Stay quiet.' And by quiet she meant, like, not loud like I used to be. People don't notice visually quiet people – that's how she used to put it. Visually, she said. She always used big words.

But now she's not here. And the phone just rang in the hall and it was Sarah's mum to say not to come today but to come tomorrow or the next day cos Sarah's sister was gonna be arriving soon from Canada like either today or maybe tomorrow. And that Sarah hasn't woken up yet. She hasn't moved at all. This is so shit. Even my mum said it was so shit.

19

Sarah

Day Three – 1 p.m.

The next time the sound came back it is a different day.

I think my brother was in my room again last night.

I don't know.

I don't know what's real.

The victim liaison officer has obviously wound up my mother about the credit cards. They are all in my room and to the accompaniment of my own personal life-support symphony, my mother has now decided that somehow her savings – not even mine, hers – are going to be hacked into. Mrs Brannon is talking in that reassuring voice in the way that she does, and my mother is badgering my dad in the way that she does, and he's not really listening, or he can't hear her because he's turned his hearing aid down. And the conversation is one big circle that keeps going round and round ... 'No, they won't have access to your bank account. Why would they? Yes, Sarah's bank account has been frozen. Yes, we can find out if they've used the cards. Yes, the bank will be insured for that. No they don't have access to your bank account ...'

I'm sure I should remember more about my mother but there was no one standing next to my dad as he watched me jump in and out of the paddling pool. 'Daddy, watch me. Daddy.' In the garden behind the house with the yellow door there was a neat little lawn. He stands there patiently, in his beige slacks and his tweed jacket and his polished lace-up shoes, beside our white-painted garden gate. The lawn was bordered by flowerbeds, a metre wide down each side and along a wooden fence at the back. They were stuffed with heavy-headed chrysanthemums, too many of them, yellow and red and orange all mixed up together. They were tied with green twine, just below their heads, and the stems strain against spindly canes. In the smallest gust of wind the canes come loose, and the flowers fall flat on the grass, exhausted.

Along the garage wall there was a trellis with an apple tree trained along it. There were tiny apples hanging from its narrow branches, cute cartoon apples that were pink and shiny. But we weren't allowed to eat them. Not ever. Bees would busy themselves in the leaves, adding a droning backdrop to the heat of the afternoon. Occasionally they would disappear into a deep black hole in the side of an apple and everything would go quiet. Their tails would poke out, vibrating silently.

In the centre of the lawn is my yellow and blue paddling pool. The tiny waves in the water are creating a glittering light show, like in a fairy story. The water is perfectly cool. I have a neon orange swimsuit that has a flowery skirt and a yellow plastic belt.

The swimsuit has got wet. It is itchy and loose and long.

The water from the pool has spilt onto the grass and made it flat and slippery. And the water has got dirty with blades of brown grass floating in the top, circling slowly, and mud and stones washing around the bottom. The gate to the garden is empty. My dad has gone. A different man is standing in the garden. An old man with torn clothes and bent hands. Dirty fingernails.

The sun goes in.

My memories come like stuttering films among a background of voices, half dream half thought. Nurses. Doctors. Cleaners. Dappled sunlight. A warm breeze. Somewhere there's music playing.

Then the lights go out.

My daydreams disappear and the voices switch off – like a radio – and I feel like I'm sinking and sinking and sinking. Swallowed up by nothingness. Sinking is beginning to feel comfortable. A safer place. I'm tired.

Tired.

This is me thinking.

I'm dying. Would that be such a bad thing?

From far away I hear the sound of a buzzer. And footsteps. There's an argument. Someone is saying, 'You can't come in. I don't care who you are.'

A door slams.

The buzzer sounds again.

'If you don't go away, I will call the police. Security are already on their way up. And I mean it.'

More footsteps. Men talking. A woman. Beth maybe.

'Alright, Sarah? It's all OK. Come on now. You're causing us all sorts of fun and games here. So you may as well come back and help us sort them out. Good night, love.'

20

Kelly

Day Four – 11 a.m.

My phone went off last night. Like in the middle of the night or something.

Message.

Unknown number.

HEY KELLY. HOPE THIS IS YOU. NO NEWS FROM HERE. SORRY. WE ARE LOOKING AFTER SARAH WELL. BTW WHAT DOES SARAH'S BROTHER LOOK LIKE?

And then, just as I was about to reply, another message.

IT'S BETH FROM THE HOSPITAL BY THE WAY. NURSE HODDER.

Beth, the nice nurse.

So I thought, well, what a strange fucking message. I replied back straight away because it was the middle of the night, right, so it must be something important.

HI BETH. IT'S KELLY. I'M FINE. SAY HI TO SARAH FOR ME. SHE DOESN'T HAVE A BROTHER. SISTER. NOT A BROTHER.

And then I lay awake for the rest of the night because I can never get back to sleep once I've woken up. I was gonna tidy my room but then I did my nails instead.

My mum woke up at like fucking dawn or something when the hospital called saying it was alright to visit Sarah. It was the tea-and-tampons lady. Said that Sarah's family are in seeing the medical team and that my mum should come in and talk to Sarah to help with the memories and shite, which I'm pretty sure doesn't fucking work but what the fuck.

So we are waiting in the fucking tragic Family Room again, with the OAP plastic chairs. And my mum is making us tea in the disgusting mugs.

It's a bit like going to a wedding or a funeral or something, visiting people in hospital. Everyone is like really, really happy or really fucking sad or just really, really nervous. No one seems to know how to behave or what to wear. My mum has got her church coat on again and her matching handbag. People like totally avoid each other's eyes.

The nurse comes in – the other one, Lucinda she's called. Beth wasn't there. She gives me a wink and says we should go on in now after all our waiting. So we walk down the faded grey plastic lino (at least it's an honest colour), which seems to go on for ever and now I'm thinking I don't really want to go in and see my friend, probably my best friend, looking like she's nearly dead. And then we are standing outside the door. My mum opens it.

'OMG, Mum, that's never her,' I say, staring at the bed with my hand over my mouth.

'Is there ever a situation, Kelly Louise Jane McCarthy, when you don't feel the need to say OMG?'

She's looking at me, not through the door.

'Oh my good lord,' she says, staring at the bed as we back out of the room again.

We're still in the corridor with the faded grey plastic lino and I'm shaking. And my mum is blowing her nose and her tissue is smearing her lipstick down her chin.

'Mum, she looks like a mummy. She looks like an Egyptian mummy.'

'I wouldn't have known her. Would you have known her?' My mum's accent is always more Irish when she's nervous. She had to give a speech once in assembly about the Christmas Table Top Fair and no one could understand a fucking word of what she said. I just said same name, no relation.

'Her eyes are all like puffed up,' I say. 'She looks like she's done ten rounds in a boxing ring.'

'They said we can't talk about anything negative in front of her, Kelly,' she hisses at me as we edge into the room. 'She might be able to hear us.'

I don't know what I was expecting a life-support machine to look like. I guess on those police programmes and hospital soaps they always look kind of clean and sterile. This doesn't look clean or sterile. There are plastic tubes snaking around everywhere. They are ridged like the bendy bit on straws. There are like TV screens either side of the bed with graphs on and numbers flashing. And there's a big machine thing that makes this clicking noise all the time. Probably it is all like totally the way it's supposed to be, but the puffy purple body lying in the bed with the bloody bandages is making it look raw and it smells too hot even though it's cold. The bed is propped up and Sarah's head is resting on a pillow. On a good day it would be a perfect angle for like reading a book. Or having a cup of tea. There are bandages all around her shaved head and a bit over her eyes. There's a piece of like blue tape holding a pipe in her open mouth. She's wearing a pale-blue hospital overall that's not her style at all. It's got like little bunches of flowers on it. She'd be well pissed off by that. Then there's a clip kind of attached to her head with a wire coming out and another smaller yellow tube going up her nose. Her eyes are so swollen and purple she wouldn't be able to open them even if she was awake.

'Well, Mum,' I say, 'she certainly don't look like she can hear us.'

'Shhh,' she whispers. 'Exactly how many people have you ever seen in a coma, then, Kelly?'

'She just looks like, like she's asleep,' I whisper back. Or dead, I think, but I don't say that.

'She is asleep. But her brain might be awake or something, so we need to talk nice to her.'

This is so mental. There is nothing to say.

'Well, go on then.' My mum is silently crying.

'What shall I say?' I don't know why we are whispering.

'I don't know. Say, "Hi Sarah. It's Kelly here." '

'That sounds like I'm on a fucking walkie-talkie. Ten-four, Sarah. Come in, Sarah. Over and out.'

'Do you think that's helping, Kelly? Go on then. What are you waiting for?'

'Hi, Sarah. It's Kelly here.' I say this loudly in case she can hear.

'There you are! That wasn't so bad.' My mum is back to whispering.

'Now what?'

'Well, just say what you've been up to. What you've been doing at school.'

'OMG, Mum, what the fuck would she want to know that for? She's in a coma. And anyway, I haven't even been to school.'

'Kelly, I don't think I need to remind you about *your language please!*'

'Hi, Sarah. It's Brenda here.' She pauses and then says, 'Also.'

'OM fucking G, Mum. What's with the "also"? Who says stuff like that – except a complete moron?'

'Well, in case she wondered who I was, you know. Since she obviously can't see us.'

And back at full volume she says, 'Billy is doing lovely in the school play, Sarah.'

'Mum, why are you shouting?'

'He's got a lovely voice. Voice of an angel, Mr Sertin says. Doesn't he, Kelly?'

'Yeah, right, Mum. Sure he says that. Exactly that.'

'Hmmph,' says my mum, more to herself. 'I'm going to find some tea.'

When my mum has gone I lean closer to Sarah, even if all that fucking disgusting yellow watery stuff that's coming through the bandages above her eyes is making me feel like I'm gonna puke.

'OMG, Sarah. Sarah! Fuck's sake. You have to wake up. This wasn't sposed to happen.'

21

Sarah

Day Four – 2 p.m.

'Afternoon, Sarah. It's Monday. I'm on a late today. But I'm full of the joys of spring. I hear Brenda and Kelly came for a visit this morning? That's nice of them. And how are you feeling? The weather is shite by the way. Wet and cold. No good for my knees.'

I'm very well, thanks, Beth. I'm beginning to like Beth. I'm beginning to get used to the routine. I like the way we have become more informal with each other even though we haven't officially met.

'It's important for you to get moving, Sarah. Sarah. You're in hospital. You've been here since Friday morning – well, Thursday night. We need to see some action now.'

Yeah, yeah, yeah. If only it were that easy.

'Plus it's that special time of day when you get down with Mr Motivator.'

I didn't know what she was talking about when she said this yesterday. Now I remember some breakfast TV show where a man in a peaked cap used to yell at the viewers to get off their fat arses. Apparently this is my morning routine. Either Beth or Lucinda or Lisa oversee my morning routine. Not that I do anything. I wish. By the strain in their voices they are rolling me around. How hideous is that? This is what they do for coma patients. Rolling over happens three times from midnight to dawn, to stop bedsores. Sponge baths and motion exercises are every morning. Proper baths I think they said are twice a week – I'm actually quite glad I won't see myself going through that. I'd actually die of embarrassment. A man came in to talk to my parents about splints to stop the legs going into a foetal position – THE legs, they don't feel like MY legs any more – but I'm not quite sure how that happens. A physiotherapist introduced himself too, to do yet another assessment and he told my parents that the comatose are likely to get pneumonia, bowel obstruction from lack of dietary fibre, urinary tract infections, blood clots in the legs, seizures, a ruptured stomach, skin breakdowns, skin infections due to lack of circulation and all the rest. They take no prisoners, these medical types. The comatose, he said. Not your daughter who is here in a coma. They try to remove the physical from the emotional. I can't tell you how removed I feel from the physical.

Hence, my personal guardian angels are warding off the impending dangers. My teeth are cleaned morning and night and I get Vaseline applied to my lips. The bandages on my eyes have been removed – and, according to Lisa, I have two 'dirty great black eyes'. My mother thinks I have the look of a lout – 'Which, by the way, is totally normal for where she lives,' she says. All this I have overheard, in between finding out about Lucinda's tree-surgeon boyfriend, Lisa's three-pound weight loss (with her leggings still presumably wedged up her arse) and Beth's developing varicose veins. Mr Malin apparently has a 'fuck-ugly' wife. My mother is a 'right royal pain in the arse' and my dad is a 'cutie' – good old Dad. I am getting used to the routine, which is a worry in itself. But I'm awake enough, aware enough to think I must be getting better.

They keep talking about the man who's been here. The man by my bed. My brother. I keep hearing snippets. Whenever the door opens, a tumble of sentences wafts into my room. My mother and father arrive.

'What do you mean? Sarah hasn't got a brother!'

I think my mother is talking to Lisa.

'I know, I know. But the thing is, Mrs Beresford, I thought she did. So if he's not her brother, who is he?'

'Who?'

Yes, who is he?!

'The man who was here! Sarah's brother.'

'She's never had a brother. Has she, Brian?'

I've never had a brother. Jesus. Who is it then? What does he want? Is this the man who mugged me?

'I think my wife is trying to work out who you thought *was* Sarah's brother? When did you see him, dear?'

'He was here before you came. On the first night. He was really concerned. He was pacing up and down and everything.'

'Where was he pacing?'

'He was just outside the ward. By the entrance. You have to buzz to get in. But he hadn't buzzed. I've told the police. He was outside, on the first night. He said he was Sarah's brother. But I didn't let him in because, well, because on the first night you have to get things straight, you know? Clear up. Get the patient comfortable. If you know what I mean. And Beth said, I mean, Nurse Hodder told me to say he couldn't come in, and to take his number, and that we would call him. But when I asked him for his number, he just ran off. I've told the police.'

Lisa, you are so stupid.

'Well, that could have been anyone, couldn't it, Brian?'

'Yes, you must have been mistaken. Perhaps there's another Sarah.'

'*Is* there another Sarah, dear?'

'No, he meant this Sarah. He came back, you see.'

He meant me.

'What do you mean, he came back?'

'He came back. The next night. When I came in to do the midnight checks, he was sitting next to the bed. Right next to the bed. He was talking to Sarah. I think he was. He was tapping the bedframe with a pen.'

Tap, tap-tap, tap.

'The same man?'

'The same, Mrs Beresford. I'm terribly sorry. The man, Sarah's brother, came back on Saturday night. He got in somehow.'

'It's not her brother. She hasn't got a brother.' *My dad is getting annoyed.* 'Can't you stop calling him that!'

The door opens.

'Lisa, you're needed at Reception. Mr and Mrs Beresford, I'm so sorry. Lisa has told you the situation, obviously. There has been a serious lapse of security, I realise. But please accept our apologies. We have full-time security on the door now. Two policemen twenty-four hours a day. And the good thing about all this is that Sarah is fine.'

After a long pause and a heavy sigh, my father replies.

'She doesn't look it, nurse, does she? Does she?'

Someone is trying to kill me.

The lift doors of my mind rattle shut. Bang. Going down.

You know those near-death scenes you get in films? The bits that are supposed to be heaven or something. You know, when someone is unconscious or in a coma and it suddenly cuts to puffy white clouds – or a desert island under a surreal purple sky dotted with diamond stars – or a field of golden barley blowing in a warm afternoon breeze. Harps are usually playing. Or violins. That is not what it's like. It's not like that at all.

This is like being in a prison cell that you can't see or touch or smell. No walls. No floor. Nothing to walk around or sleep on or pee into. Do you think people in a prison cell can even conceive that there is a worse place? This is a worse place. It has to be worse, right?

There are different levels of nothingness. The worst is the black place. I'm gonna call it the Black Place, where there are no dreams and no sounds and no memories. Just blackness. The bottom of the lagoon. One up from that is the Muffled Place where I can hear something but can't quite make it out. I can dream there. I can think. And when I dream, I forget myself. I almost think the dream is real. Then I can remember what it feels like to feel. I've been to the beach running in and out of the cold shallows, feeling the wind in my face and through my hair. I've sat behind my desk in the office and looked through my post. I've lain on my bed under the bay window and watched the sun's patterns on the embroidered cover become longer and darker until they disappear. The dreams usually end when the volume goes back up, when I can hear the nurses chatting or my family. My dad. My mother.

Locked-in syndrome. I read a book about it once. About a man who worked on a magazine and had a heart attack and was locked in for months before anyone noticed that he was trying to communicate with his eyes or something. Locked in is right. Locked in. With no door. Jesus, I could be here for years.

When I can hear, I allow myself to be optimistic, that I can – no, that I will – make a finger twitch or open my eyes or scrunch my nose. But when I'm in the Black Place I almost wish that I could end all this. It's so unfair. How did it happen? Who could have done this? Some dirty kid, probably off his head on weed or crack, has stolen my life. I want to howl from the pit of my stomach. I can't even do that.

I've remembered more about my mother. I remember she always felt closed off to me. Maybe she just preferred my sister. I was my dad's favourite. I remember coming home from school with a painting and holding it up for her to see and she said how nice it was, but she hadn't actually looked. She hadn't actually lifted her eyes from the meal she was cooking. I remember telling her my exam results and her saying that I was getting far too big-headed and I should watch it or I wouldn't be able to get through the doors. When I came top in English she said, 'Oh no, here comes The Big I Am.' I don't think she liked me. Not at all. I can't remember her ever hugging me. Or kissing me goodnight. Not like my dad. I can just remember her telling my dad that I was spoilt. By him. While he was standing behind her shrugging and winking.

We moved when I was seven. From the house with the yellow door. To a bigger house with no garden. My mother didn't want a garden, she said. Too much trouble with gardeners, she said. And my father said he totally agreed. And that shut her up. I said that I was glad because I didn't like gardeners anyway. And she hissed that dirty little liars grow into dirty big liars so why didn't I just stop whining on? Just because I was pretty, she said, didn't give me the right to tell lies. And I remember my dad saying that he was glad to see the back of Mr Eades, and my mother saying that 'he was a good man, there was no doubting that, everybody said so', as she stared hard at me.

When I was much older I went to visit my parents. There was a man with me. Adam? My mother said she would make fish pie for dinner. I like fish pie, only she uses really horrible fish. Cheap fish. Tasteless mush. Carol was there. Carol. My sister. I have a sister.

I remember her pouring us a glass of wine each, for courage, she'd said. She knew. So we sat on the sofa in the sitting room – it was a lavender-pink velour sofa with stubby pine legs that sunk so low into the pink nylon carpet that the whole thing seemed to be floating. The wine was kept in the cabinet at the far end of the room, the mobile drinks bar – that's what my mother called it. The cabinet had a mirrored pull-down door that turned into a shelf for preparing the drinks. The gin bottle that had stood in there for years must by then have been made up of 99 per cent water, diluted after so many times of us sneaking a glass and refilling it from the tap. My parents didn't drink gin. Port and lemon and sherry were my mother's favourites.

The wine was white and warm. From the edge of my seat, and with my wine glass (free from the Esso garage) in hand, I delivered the news that we were getting married. My mother was reading People's Friend magazine. I remember thinking it was a rather odd title for someone of my mother's disposition. She was wearing a navy and white ensemble – a white tie-neck blouse from her Margaret Thatcher days and a woollen pleated skirt. Her hair was newly permed and sprayed into a neat globe of black curls. She must have picked the magazine up at the hairdresser's. With her head to one side, she kept licking her third finger then flicking the page. Lick finger, flick page. Lick finger, flick page, as though I had said nothing at all worth considering. As though someone she didn't even know had mentioned something terribly dull about the weather. Afterwards Carol told me that my mother had said, 'I don't know what she wants to marry him for.' We went back to London. Then all I remember is a hole in my kitchen door. A hole the size of a fist. With splinters of wood on the brown carpet. And blood in the sink. Not my blood. Adam's blood.

There's no one in my room now. Just me and my machines. The relative peace is shattered by Mr Malin and his students. Malin *is one of the few people who generally practises what he preaches when it comes to speaking in front of me. His voice tends to be so low that I can't quite make out what he says. This time he is less discreet. He has the results of my latest brain scan. He says he's got to talk my parents through it later. Yesterday he'd said, 'Let's look forward to some progress, shall we?' and my parents had perked up.*

He is asking one of the students to assess the scan.

'Although I would say, sir, that there is too much swelling to get a definitive answer, but I believe that the scan suggests that she is in a persistent vegetative state, unaware of either herself or her environment. She may have sleep cycles and awake cycles. But since she has no voluntary responses to sound, light, motion, and no understanding of language as well as no control of her bowel or bladder functions, I would put her chances of recovery at very slim.'

Malin responds but I can't hear.

'Sir, I would simply explain to them that recovery is rare.'

That was the student again.

'Ten out of ten, Miss James.'

Ten out of ten – that's what Malin said.

This is me thinking.

Shit.

Shit, shit, shit, shit.

I just have no strength for this.

Oh, listen to yourself. You are not getting better. You are not going to get better. You are better off dead anyway.

I was in the Black Place earlier. Maybe yesterday. Before Malin gave me the prognosis. It was cold, so cold. The bottom of the lagoon. Down that deep, you would be cold, wouldn't you? I was plucked out of the darkness, catapulted back to the present by this voice whispering right in my ear. I don't know how I could have forgotten – it sounded so urgent, so desperate.

'OMG, Sarah. Sarah! Fuck's sake. You have to wake up. This wasn't sposed to happen.'

My heart starts pumping really fast. I can hear the blood rushing around my body. And then I remember Kelly.

22

Kelly

Day Four – 3 p.m.

We're in the hospital cafeteria. We had lunch here. Cheese and bacon grilled baguettes. Quite nice. Must come here more often. Joke. Sarah hasn't woken up but apparently after we left they removed some of the bandages and Lucinda says she looks a lot less like a cartoon mummy. But still not like her. Not yet, she said. She ain't pretty.

The cafeteria has got like a glass ceiling. It's at the front of the hospital. My mum says it's called an atrium. If you sit in a sunny bit it's really hot and if you sit in a shady bit it's really cold. There are automatic doors out the front that swish open every time someone gets within like a fucking mile of them even if they aren't coming in, so there's wind blowing in all the time too, big bursts of cold wind mixed up with the smell of cigarettes and clouds of dust off the pavement. Outside there're people smoking their heads off. In wheelchairs, some of them. With drips.

Seriously. Why would you smoke if you've got a drip? It's like they're not dying enough already.

There's this old man standing right by the door, crying. He keeps dabbing his face with a big crumpled-up hanky that is filthy. He's got a thick woolly old coat on, even though it's not exactly winter outside, and then his pyjamas and his slippers. And he keeps just looking at the ceiling. Like there's something really interesting up there. Maybe he's just been told he's like gonna die of something, really soon. And he's looking for heaven. Like maybe he's got lung cancer, right? Or maybe he just got here and they've told him that his wife went and died in the night or something. He wouldn't be in his pyjamas and his slippers if he just got here. Unless he came on the bus in his pyjamas and his slippers cos his wife's not at home any more to remind him to put his clothes on. Maybe he just went out the front for a fag. What I wouldn't do for a fag right now. But I don't smoke any more. Sarah said not to smoke. She said it's not nice to smoke. Well, she said people think it's not nice to smoke. She said the baddies in movies always have a fag in their hand. She said you can always tell whodunnit by who smokes.

I was only like halfway down my chocolate milkshake and smoky bacon Walkers, when I saw Sarah's parents come in through the automatic doors. It didn't seem right to be stuffing my face. They joined the end of the self-service queue and you could see by the way that they kept looking over at us that they couldn't decide whether to come and sit down or like go and sit on their own. And then my mum did one of them gross embarrassing waves, that way that old people wave, so they came over. The groany noise the chair legs made on the tiled floor as they dragged them out from under the table made me jump. I thought it was them making the noise. Seriously. I'm not even lying. The noise matched the looks on their faces. I feel sorry for them. Sorry that their daughter is sick. Sorry that they didn't even seem to know her.

'What was Sarah like when she was little?' I say to Mr Beresford, when my mum and Sarah's mum get talking about medical stuff.

'She was the most beautiful girl,' he says, and his eyes are like wet and twinkly. And I think 'holy fuck, I really hope he isn't gonna cry' cos I was only asking to be polite.

'She was such an ugly baby, though, wasn't she, Brian?' joins in Mrs Beresford, who, like my mum, can follow two conversations at the same time.

And I can see my mum's lips get tight and she shifts her butt in her chair, and I can tell she's thinking that you don't speak ill of the ... ill?

'We used to hide her face inside a bonnet so that no one would see her.' She is grinning like a false grin even though her eyes are red from crying. She has mascara smudged down her cheek and a smear of orange lipstick on her front teeth.

'She was the light of my life,' says Mr Beresford, quietly, like he's just talking to me. 'She used to laugh all the time. She was such a happy child.'

'She was full of herself when she was little,' says Mrs Beresford. My mum flashes me a look that says 'here we fucking go'.

'She won a competition, didn't she, Brian? A beauty competition when she was three.'

'Little Miss Pears,' says Mr Beresford, stirring his coffee absent-mindedly. 'She looked like an angel.' He's also now gazing at the ceiling. I just double-check to make sure there isn't actually something quite interesting up there.

'I always found her quiet,' says my mum. 'I think they call it unassuming.'

'Yes, she turned into a bit of a bookworm. I don't know where she got that from,' says Mrs Beresford. 'I don't ever read myself. Haven't the time. But she always had her head in a book. If we lost her we'd find her in the airing cupboard, lying on one of the bottom shelves reading Enid Blyton or something with fairies and princesses.'

'It was school that quietened her down,' says Mr Beresford, still looking at the ceiling and seeming sad again.

'What're you all talking about?' says a woman who suddenly drags a chair up to the table. You couldn't mistake Sarah's sister. She looks so similar. Not as pretty. Not as thin as Sarah had got. But same genes. She's wearing a leather jacket. Fucking nice leather jacket. And one of those scarves that models wear. Those fucking expensive ones. Cashminas or something. It's lilac blue.

'Carol, you're here,' says Mrs Beresford, leaning over and kissing her.

Mr Beresford stands up to give her a hug and there's this well awkward bit when we don't know whether we should get up or stay sitting.

'This is our eldest daughter, Carol – she lives in Canada,' says Mrs Beresford to my mum. 'She just arrived yesterday.'

'Glad to meet you,' says my mum. My mum looks at me like I'm a total spaz and I say, 'Hello, I'm Kelly', and she nods and smiles. She's only a bit older than Sarah and quite a lot like her to look at.

Mr Beresford is hurriedly putting his hands in his pockets and pulling out hankies and a wallet and a diary, looking for some change.

'Do you want a coffee, Carol?' he says.

'Yes, please, Dad. Do they do cappuccino?' she says.

'It's very milky. Full-fat milk,' Mrs Beresford says. 'You won't want all that milk, will you?'

'Cappuccino, please, Dad,' she continues, smiling a bright smile. 'And a packet of crisps, please.' She winks at me, looking down at my half-eaten packet.

Poor-old-bastard Mr Beresford trails off to get the coffee, joining the back of the queue he just left. And Carol launches into this interrogation about like totally everything the doctor has said, and the nurses have said, and how does Sarah seem, and all that. And Carol writes notes in a small leather notebook that matches her scarf. And when her coffee arrives she looks up at me and says, 'So, Kelly. What have you got to say?' Funny really. She doesn't mean it properly, you know, like she doesn't really think I've got anything to say. She's just trying to be nice, I spose. Join me in the 'adult' conversation. She's the only person to actually properly ask me anything. Out of all these people, the police and the nurses and Mrs Tea and Tampons, who just assume that I won't know anything cos I'm a bit of a twat or a kid or something, the one person to ask me anything is someone who doesn't know anything about me at all. 'Oh, I don't know,' I say. And my mum goes, 'She never says anything much.' And I give her a look that means fuck off, Mum. She winks back. She's funny, my mum. She totally gets me sometimes. Ever since she asked Sarah for help, I've been much more in control of my life. In control of what I say and how I say it. Making choices for me rather than just reacting to the choices other people were making. I think I only realised that just around the time that the school got burnt down.

My mum wants to go home. She keeps swivelling her eyes towards the door and thinks no one else can see her doing it. She'd said we'd have to go if Carol arrived. And Carol wants to see Sarah like right away. My mum decides she needs the loo. She goes in the disabled cos there's a queue. Why are there always queues in women's toilets? While I'm waiting outside holding onto her fucking ridiculous beige handbag, I see Nurse Hodder. She's just standing there, in the corridor, staring at a printout. When she sees me she blushes slightly. Weird, right? Then she walks towards me. My mum is still in the loo.

'Hi,' she says. 'Can you have a look at this for me?'

It's a photo of a man, from CCTV. The printout is rubbish. The ink has smudged. It looks like the entrance to the hospital. The time on it says 23:39. 14.03.2014. Last Friday.

'I dunno,' I say. 'Could be anyone.'

The man has black hair. Curly. He's wearing a parka with a fur hood. He looks about thirty, I spose. His clothes don't look like old clothes. It's hard to tell.

'This is the man who says he's Sarah's brother,' she says.

'Well, it's not, cos she doesn't have one, right?'

'No. I know. But I wondered if you recognised him.'

'I don't know who he is,' I say. Cos I don't.

And the more I look at him the more he looks like Adam. I start to feel sick.

'What's the matter with you?' she says.

'You've turned green. Are you alright?'

'It looks like Adam,' I say.

'He's dead, Kelly,' she says.

'I know,' I say, and then pause. 'Are you sure?'

'Yes, I'm sure he is,' she replies and puts her arm around my shoulders.

'Do you believe in ghosts, Beth?'

Beth looked at me strange. And blinked.

23

Sarah

Day Four – 5 p.m.

It was Kelly who hissed in my ear. I remember her. The girl from next door. Blond hair. Or was it brown? Brenda's girl. And I remember the first time I saw her. I was less than impressed. I was in this Victorian house. My house, I guess? It had a newly painted white wooden gate and a privet hedge. The upstairs bedroom had no carpet and the furniture was stacked against one wall, with cardboard boxes piled up against the other. There were no curtains either, and I was looking out of the window over the street where I could see just around the bend. It was about four o'clock – home time – so the street was full of mothers pushing prams and dragging toddlers, and straggling kids in no hurry to get home. It was a summer afternoon with no breeze and the sky felt heavy. A storm was threatening. A blond girl, who was actually twelve but could have been ten years older judging by the state of her, was eating crisps, just by the corner before she turned into our final stretch of street. She had over-bleached and ironed her hair to the point that it wafted in the non-existent breeze. She was over-made-up too. I wondered what kind of mother would let her daughter out looking like a wannabe hooker, and what kind of school would let that pass for uniform. She was holding the hand of a small blond boy, who looked like she might have done before the war paint got the better of her. I guessed he was her brother. He must have been about five. The air felt dense and their conversation was muffled. But they seemed to be having a joke about something. He had a pink lollipop. Suddenly from nowhere, she pulled at his arm. From nowhere. The senseless aggression was completely shocking. It's the way you see those EDL skinheads yank at the leads of their godforsaken dogs. Her hair flew in a ragged curtain across her screwed-up face. The boy was called Billy, I remember. He didn't shout out. He just started to cry, his lollipop back in his mouth. Is there anything more tragic than seeing someone cry when they're eating a lollipop? Without either of them saying anything at all, she continued around the corner, whereupon a middle-aged woman appeared like a bat out of hell and scooped him up. I stepped back from the window. I didn't want to be seen by her. Or Kelly.

Next time I saw Brenda was when she introduced herself over the garden wall that separated our front paths. My new next-door neighbour. I didn't say anything. About Kelly, I mean. She talked about her clever daughter. I hoped there was rather more to her than met the eye. Or perhaps rather less.

I am snapped back into reality by the sound of loud voices. My room seems to be full of people.

'Why didn't you tell me about that when I got here?'

This is my sister. I'd know her voice anywhere. My sister is here. I know my sister. Her name is Carol and she's older than me and much braver. Always was. I didn't realise she had come. God, things must be bad.

'If some strange man has been in her room, why didn't you tell me straight away?'

'Because, Carol, we were talking with Brenda.'

God, they're all here.

'And? What difference does that make?'

'We don't want everyone knowing our business. Do we, Brian? Brian?'

'No, June, but that's not the point. The point is, he's gone now. The police are here. They've got a photo of him. Let's leave all that to them. We should be looking after Sarah. Helping to bring her back. Talk to her, they said.'

'But, Dad, it's not working, is it?'

'Mr Malin is her consultant and he says that we just need to talk to her.'

'Well, Mum, let's get Mr Malin in here. Let's see what else this hospital can do. Like maybe some medical tests.'

'We don't want any trouble, Carol. Brian, tell Carol we don't want any trouble. Brian!'

'Trouble? Mum, we're already in trouble. This is about as big as trouble can be. Don't you get it? Can't you understand that we have to do something now?'

I love it when she flips. She has always flipped. She's the outspoken one. Up until she was about seven she was in charge because she was always first at everything. She could tie her shoelaces, she could read, she could write, she could play cards. Once she got locked in the cupboard at the top of the stairs by the older kids from opposite – only once, because she nearly broke Helen's and Alexa's legs when she got out. I could never fight back. Because I was smaller. I got locked in the cupboard all the time. Then, one day, I wanted to play with her and she wouldn't let me. She said I was a baby and I didn't know how to play. She laughed. I cried. She ignored me. So I went downstairs. Next thing, my mother comes upstairs and wallops her around the head. 'Don't lock your sister in the cupboard,' screams my mother. 'I didn't,' she shouts back. 'She's a liar,' she says. My mother just hit her again in the exact same place she'd just hit her and slammed the door. I was about five. I was waiting for a thump that never came. 'Well done,' she said. 'You've got balls.' She let me play with her from then on.

'SARAH, ADAM'S DEAD.'

She is yelling. I guess most coma victims don't get treated like that. Someone starts to cry.

'Carol, that's enough!'

That's my dad. He never raises his voice. Never.

'Dad. It's not working, all this nice chatting stuff. Is it? Don't you think that we have to try everything to get her out of this? Happy memories? Doesn't work. Surprise, surprise. Telling her you love her? Doesn't work. So how about this? SARAH – YOU ARE GONNA DIE IF YOU DON'T WAKE UP, SO FUCKING WAKE UP.'

That's balls.

I was still thinking about Kelly when I got an image of this man, one hand on a lamp post propping himself up. It's dark. His knees are bent and he's leaning forwards, and with his other hand he's leaning on his knee, and his head is dropped forward like he is going to be sick. I can't see his face behind the thick black curls but I know it must be Adam. Then he looks up into the distance like he is looking for something way off. Not me, though. Probably he is just trying to see straight. He pushes his hand against his thighs and slowly levers himself upright and steadies himself with the lamp post. There is a can of Special Brew poking out of the pocket of his black coat and an empty one by his feet.

This is Adam. I'm sure of it.

It is Adam, but it's not the Adam I married.

24

Kelly

Day Four – 6 p.m.

I didn't tell my mum about the photo. Or anything at all about the man in Sarah's room. I don't tell my mum a lot of things. She worries too much.

Beth says it's a coincidence that it looks like Adam. Says my eyes are playing tricks on me. But she doesn't know Adam. And if his brother is anything like him, he will be up to no fucking good.

My mum says we can't go and visit Sarah again until her mum and dad call us. She said that the family would want to be together with Sarah and that we weren't family. I said we were Sarah's proper family but my mum said people like them didn't see it that way. We drove down Wood Green High Street and I just stared out of the window. It all looked different. I used to be like, 'What's in Top Shop?' or 'Who's in Caffè Nero?' but now it all seems strange.

Before I knew Sarah I used to bunk school all the time, to go to like TK Maxx or wherever. Or down McDonald's even though half the time we'd only just got to school and we weren't even hungry. I've never bunked school to sit in a hospital for like EVER, waiting for a coma to wear off. I think Sarah would approve. She'd say I've turned into a fucking angel. Well, she wouldn't say 'fucking'. She'd say I'm an angel, at least I look like one from the outside.

Before I met Sarah I said 'pacific' instead of 'specific'. I also said 'random', 'totally', 'spaz', 'weird', and 'something' with a k on the end. Actually I said 'somefink' with an f and a k. And I said 'fuck' a lot. Out loud, I mean – in your head doesn't count. Sarah said words like 'coincidentally' and 'furthermore' and 'good grief', which made me laugh. It made her laugh when I said 'pacific', especially when she corrected me and I said there was no such fucking word as 'specific' and that everyone knew it started with a p.

It was all a bit awkward when I first went round. My mum said that Sarah had invited me for tea. But I knew that was bullshit. I mean it's totally random for your neighbour who is like twice as old as you are to invite you round for tea when you don't even like fucking tea. My mum said I should watch out for her car and when she got inside her house Sarah would put the kettle on. I'm totally not big on tea. I like Coke or chocolate milkshake or energy drinks. But although I knew it was all a bit of a set-up, I waited until her car was outside her house and I knocked on her front door. It's funny seeing the inside of someone's house when it's the same as yours only they've done it different. My mum has this spongy white wallpaper in her hall, well, it's all over the house, actually, that's got spirals on that I trace with my finger whenever I'm listening outside the front room. You can see a grey patch just by the light switch where my forehead has been leaning against it. And my mum has green carpet everywhere except in the hall cos that's where Billy leaves his bike, unless he's left it out the back again. And not in the bathroom cos she says it would rot the amount of water I get all over everywhere. Anyway, Sarah's house is grey downstairs. Grey painted walls that aren't shiny and apparently that's the whole point. It's a funny grey. Sort of nearly green. She says she doesn't really like green but Adam does. The hallway has these black and white tiles like they have in them posh stately homes and there are grey carpets in the room that Sarah calls the lounge but Adam says it's called a sitting room.

Anyway, she made the tea and I pretended that I always have tea and put seven spoons of sugar in because she didn't have any sugar cubes and then actually it was a bit more disgusting than it usually is. And then she asked me how I was getting on. Just that – 'How are you getting on?' And you know how sometimes that is like totally the wrong thing to say to someone, cos then they ask themselves how they are actually getting on and then they realise that they are actually getting on really, really bad. So it's not a question I ask random people cos quite often it makes them cry and you know you're gonna be in for a right long session when they haven't even started talking and they're crying. Anyway, when Sarah asked me how I was getting on, I just thought about it for like one second and then I started crying.

The thing with Wino had got worse than I ever dreamed it could. I'm not even lying. Since the day with the locker key, which I told Sarah about in serious detail, Wino had taken to picking me out. His favourite trick was to come up behind me and kind of wrap his hand around my ponytail and then yank it. "Ello, Blondie," he'd say, and I would get pulled backwards into the locker room by my hair. He even did it to Clare sometimes, thinking it was me. Twat. In the locker room the homies, who were like fourteen or fifteen, for fuck's sake, would finger their flick knives, trying to look as hard as their big brothers or their dads. Half the time I think they were pissed or stoned out of their minds or something.

Kathryn Cowell ran the school from the far corner of the locker room. There used to be a gym next door – it got turned into the canteen when the sports fields were sold to make the Rec. We don't do games now. Hardly any. Only when the minibus can be bothered to turn up to take us up the pool at Archway. Or when you are in Year 7 when they make you jump off benches and stuff, which is like totally stupid. The changing rooms became the locker room, lined with rows and rows of lockers, and hooks and wire baskets for coats and spare shoes. She had come to the school after being expelled from two other schools before. Someone said that the school PTA had tried to block her coming because they'd heard her reputation from when she was at a secondary school in Harlow New Town. But there was nothing the authorities could do that was legal because she was under sixteen and because her parents had got the law on their side. I guess this must be a different law to the police law, or that wouldn't make sense, right? My mum says it's got nothing to do with what's legal. It's to do with Kathryn's dad being an East End gangster. Mum says anyone messing with Kathryn will get their face rearranged. No one has ever tested out the theory.

Sarah said that Kathryn sounded like 'a dyed-in-the-wool bully – unfortunate in size, shape, stature and attitude'. I wrote that down so I could remember it. Sarah said 'dyed in the wool' means that she was made like that and she would never change. And I think saying 'unfortunate' is like not really being as harsh as you might be if you actually saw her cos she isn't just over-weight, she's like a massive barrel. My mum would say brick shithouse. She's quite small. Like in height she's quite short, I mean, and she walks weird cos she's got like little stocky foot-ballers' legs and she always wears them platform sneakers. Plat-form sneakers, no matter what. She has a thin mouth and a big old chin that she shoves out. Kathryn Cowell's way of dealing with her 'unfortunate physicality' – Sarah said I should never get caught slagging her off in terms she would understand – is to make herself look so much fucking worse. Her hair is shaved except for a layer on the top that is dyed white blond with a black fringe that flops to one side against the black stubbly sides. A heavy gold-coloured chain hangs from her earlobe that has grown abnormally long with all that chain, which then con-nects up to her nostril. The hole in her nostril is dragged down by the weight, making her nose look lopsided. Not that you can ever actually stare at her face for too long. This I have seen from the corner of my eye. She was sat outside Mrs Backhouse's office once when I had left my French vocab book at home for the millionth time. That's the only time I have ever seen her without her homies. Her homies are all boys – no girls, just five ugly bastards who follow her around like pitbull puppies and do all the dirty work. Dinner money, mobiles, earrings, homework, pens, packets of crisps, lip gloss, pets – there's nothing that Kathryn Cowell won't take. She randomly picks out her victims with her gang in tow, then stands right in their way, with her flat fat hand outstretched, her stubby chewed fingers beckoning impatiently. Sometimes she doesn't even say anything. She just sticks out her hand.

All this was just another fucking normal day for South Haringey Secondary School. It happened to most people. And most of the time people just caved. The kids who didn't cave, and there weren't very many of them, most often got cut. A slash on the arm or leg with plenty of blood put any wannabe heroes right off. That was the boys. The girls didn't ever stick up for themselves. Well, I guess the girls just did what they were told. Same for me.

Anyway, on this one pacific day (I still talked like that then) that Wino snagged me in the locker room, I had a new phone that my Auntie Liz had bought me. It was a new Nokia with a camera. And the last thing she'd said when I'd opened it was 'Don't lose it.' So handing it over to Kathryn Cowell was gonna be like total brain damage. (Can I say that now or is it like totally bad taste?) And Wino must've seen me cos those guys always hang out in the bike sheds way before school starts to have a fag and size up the kids with the bikes. They lean against the humanities block wall, sitting on the pavement that's pock-marked with cig butts. And while I was walking past, along the corridor by the art block, I suddenly thought, hide the fucking phone. So like a total retard I hid the fucking phone in my sock. When Kathryn Cowell's hand went out in the locker room, Wino was just like, 'Get the fucking phone out of your fucking sock, you fucking slag, or your fucking little brother fucking gets it, right?' I didn't even know he knew I had a brother. And I said, 'I don't even like my fucking brother, you fucking twat.' And he was like, 'I know where you live, bitch. I'll come round and chop your fucking ponytail off.' That's what he always said he'd do. And he took my phone out of my sock and knocked his elbow into my eye socket. What would you do if that happened to you? Tell your mum? Tell your teacher? Tell your headmistress?

Telling Sarah was the first time I'd ever talked about any of that. Even with your mates you didn't really say anything. Even when you've got a fat black eye. You just didn't say anything. At first I could see that Sarah didn't really believe me, even though I still had the remains of the black eye. I think she probably still thought I was being like dramatic about the whole thing. You probably think so too. Sarah said why didn't I go and speak to Mrs Backhouse? Or a teacher that I got on well with, like such a thing existed. I said that all the teachers knew already. Mrs Backhouse totally knew. No one said nothing. Sarah said that by the way that was a double negative and, in this situation, their silence made them complicit. I liked how she said that. I don't know if I know what it actually means but I think it means they're as fucking bad as Kathryn is. And she said I needed to be ostensibly invisible. And I didn't know what that meant either. I said, 'Does it mean not handing over my new Nokia with a camera?' And she said it meant not even being asked to hand over your new Nokia with a camera.

She said being plain means you're less likely to get hit.

My mum wants to know if we wanna go to McDonald's. There's one by the tube station that has an indoor climbing frame and ballpond and Billy likes it there. Billy's had his bath already and frankly I can't be bothered. There's a pot noodle in the cupboard. My mum usually wants to go there when she wants to talk about something. She thinks french fries make life more bearable. I told her I was tired. But really, my reception is shite in there. And if there's a message about Sarah, I want to get it straight away. I didn't tell her that, though.

25

Sarah

I've remembered more about my mother now. I think it's the repeated requests for tea. My mother has always drunk industrial quantities of tea. And here she is the same. Every five minutes she is off out of the door, hunting down a tea trolley. It reminded me of this time that my mother was sitting in the window seat of Burger King in Southwark, the one near the Register Office. It's not an obvious place to find my mother; in fact the reverse is true. I don't expect wild horses would drag her into a Burger King, not even on a good day. She was waiting for me in Burger King and I was waiting for Adam in a car outside Burger King, and my dad was pacing the road that runs down the side of the Register Office. She had a pink suit and a yellow hat with a ribbon around the edge and a matching silk flower corsage and a cup of thick American tan-coloured tea in a polystyrene cup. Her skin looked powdery white and her bright-coral lipstick was made somehow all the more vulgar for the false smile it painted.

He was always late. I knew that then.
He had a hat, like a little Chinese hat.
It was too small for his head.
I was so in love with him.

'So the doctor said what? Precisely what?'

My sister is here again.

'He said that once the medication had been reduced we may – *may*, Carol – be able to see signs of brain function. They reduced the medication once she had stabilised, on the first day. Then he said that after ten days we'd know something. Ten days. He said she may have long-term problems.'

'Precisely what long-term problems?'

She's brilliant. Always cuts to the chase.

'It's not that simple, Carol. The doctor said that it's best if we speak quietly to her, tell her how much we love her and then maybe that will wake her up.'

That's my dad.

'What is not simple about asking what the long-term problems might be?'

Silence.

'Well?'

Nothing.

'Dad.'

'I think we need to be careful what we discuss in front of Sarah, Carol. She may be able to hear us. We don't want to frighten her. We just want her to come back, don't we, June?'

'So she *can* hear then, can she? They think she *can* hear what we are saying? Did they actually say locked-in syndrome?'

'Well, she might be able to hear us, they said. Didn't they?'

'Alright then, Sarah, WAKE UP.'

If only it were that easy!

'Not like that, Carol. We've been speaking to her quietly. They said to remind her of happy memories.'

'Happy memories? What'll they be, then? When we spent a day walking around Stonehenge? When we went on a scenic drive for a week along Hadrian's sodding Wall? When, on every long car journey, we stopped in a lay-by to eat hard-boiled eggs – which nobody actually likes – ten minutes after we had left the house. Oh yeah. Happy days.'

If I could stand up and applaud I would. Although I actually do quite like hard-boiled eggs.

'Carol, you're upsetting your mother.'

'Oh right, sorry, Mother. Sarah's lying here at death's door – with no one really knowing what the fuck is going on, but perish the thought that your fucking stupid holidays were anything other than fucking dull.'

There's a silence now. Obviously my mum is crying, judging by the loud sniffs.

'I'm going to find a coffee.'

She's not. She's going to have a fag. That's what she says when she's going to have a fag. When she comes back she is still looking for a fight.

'Look. Don't you think we should be discussing what's really going on here?'

'We know what's going on here, Carol. We don't need your searing insights.'

Go, Dad.

'We don't want to have another argument about it now, do we, Brian?'

'What are you having a go at me for, June?'

'This isn't "having a go", Brian. I am merely saying that ...'

'Mum. Don't you think it's odd that Sarah is, you know, like she is? You know. Like she never says anything.'

'She says things all the time.'

'She speaks to your mother every day, Carol. Which is more than you do.'

'Yeah, she rings and never says anything. When have you ever seen her really laughing? Even at her own wedding. Did she really love Adam? When did you see her really having a good time? Letting her hair down. Or really crying? Really upset? She doesn't do extremes, does she? She's just in the middle. Not feeling anything.'

'Oh, Carol. What are you making up now?'

'I don't really know what all this has to do with Sarah, Carol. She needs our help, not your personality assassination.'

'Where were all the drunken parties and forgetting to do homework? Where were all the boyfriends?'

Boyfriends?

'Not everyone had to learn the way you did.'

'Acknowledged, Mother. Thank you so much.'

'She was just different to you. No better, no worse.'

'What about boyfriends, though? It's not like she wasn't pretty. Isn't pretty. Sorry. She went out with like four people and they were all complete bastards.'

'Who was a complete bastard?'

'Martin for a start.'

Martin?

'Which one was he?'

'You know, the hockey player. Didn't he break her wrist?'

'I don't remember anyone breaking her wrist. Brian?'

'I don't remember anyone called Martin.'

He did break my wrist. When we were walking down the street and he said a man looked at me in a funny way. In a way that meant why is a pretty girl like her going out with a knob like him. That's what he said. I never even saw the guy.

'What about that one with the red van? He was a total complete bastard.'

James.

'The one who nearly ran me over? He was an odd one.'

When I broke up with him he used to follow me everywhere. From home to school. From school to home. He would sit in his car down the road from our house all night and wait for me to leave. He did nearly run my mother over.

'Ian was a nice lad. What about that Ian?'

'You're right, Mum, he wasn't a complete bastard. He dumped her after two months. Said she was an emotional cripple.'

'He did not say that, Carol. Where do you get these stories?'

He was jealous. All the time. Who was I phoning, where was I going. He wanted to own me.

'Adam was a good man. A decent man. We always rubbed along well.'

'Dad, you never liked him. You said so from the start. Actually he was pretty much alright until he started drinking lager all day and smoking weed all night. Then he was a horror. But, you know, Sarah never said anything bad about him, did she? Not one word. He would come rolling in, in the middle of the night, and she would be cleaning up his sick and all sorts. She's just one of life's victims.'

'Maybe you've got it all wrong, Carol. Maybe you're the one who's not so perfect.'

'When did she become a victim, Mother? When did she start thinking it was OK for people to walk all over her? She doesn't *feel*, Mother. Or if she does, she doesn't say she does. She just lets people hurt her. That's different to most humans. Doesn't that bother you? She's unnatural. You can tell when most people are upset or hurt or happy. She never gives anything away. Never has. Well, she did when she was little. What happened to the bubbly little girl?'

'Don't start on with lies, Carol. We all had enough of her lies at the time.'

'Wait, what? What lies, Mum? What are you talking about? Dad, what is she talking about?'

'Why would you want to rewrite history, Carol? It's not like she's even –'

'Am I? Am I really? Rewriting history? I thought we were just trying to work out how on earth she got here.'

I don't feel anything?

I don't now.

And every time the buzzer goes I wonder if that man is coming back.

26

Kelly

Day Five – 1 a.m.

The streetlights have turned the puddles in the road dirty orange. It's raining. My phone is burning green neon. I have full signal and full battery and no fucking messages. My mum and me took Billy to Burger King and he got a kid's meal with a plastic toy in it. Billy was in his pyjamas already but nobody cared. I didn't even want to go but Mum said it would be good to get out. Trouble is you never know who is gonna turn up at that Burger King. Everyone goes there. I spent an hour trying to snap together a plastic plane with a moving propeller. It had to be moving, Billy said. It was better than staring at my phone. My mum says I ought to go to school tomorrow and fucking unbelievably I think I might. I can't stand waiting around. I'd rather be in French. LOL. The day has finally come that I'd rather be at school. What a fucking transformation that is.

The day that the languages block burnt down I got sent home from school. We all did. That was a first. Rather than bunking off they'd actually told us to go home, which is lucky cos it's what I was gonna do anyway cos it was double pottery and I haven't got any big urge to make a fucking Roman coil pot. Instead I spent the entire afternoon painting my nails with this new crackle top coat. Have you seen it? You paint your nails one colour – like, say, pink – then you put the crackle top coat on in a different colour – I did black but you can do any colour what you want – and it goes on normal then after like a minute it cracks and you can see the layer underneath. You have to let it dry, though. It doesn't explain that on the bottle. It just says put the top coat on without saying that if the bottom coat is not dry it all turns to mush and you have to start again. They ought to say that. I got it all over the fucking carpet too. So, anyway, I had these new nails at fucking last, and I was waiting for Sarah to get back so I could show her my new nails and tell her about the languages block burning down.

The languages block burning down was a typical Kathryn Cowell moment – she liked to have a few of those each year just to keep her rep up. It happened like maybe two weeks after I started meeting Sarah. I'd got quite used to seeing her most weekday evenings. It was still light enough to sit in the garden although I would always imagine my mum standing right behind the fence listening, so sometimes we'd sit in the kitchen on the kitchen units (with the back doors open), which my mum says is unhygienic. I think by this point we'd already decided to change my hair colour. It didn't take a fucking genius to work out that the reason that I was on Wino's radar was because I had a blond ponytail and that if I got rid of that maybe I'd become a little less obvious. But Sarah said I had to do it gradually. Not like one minute White Platinum and the next minute like mouse brown because she said that would draw attention to me more than staying White Platinum. And the whole point of changing was not to draw attention. She said sometimes trying to stop drawing attention to yourself can actually draw attention to yourself. She said it's like a man who wears a grey suit and a grey coat and then wears a grey shirt and a grey tie with it. She says that's all too grey and people would go why is he wearing a grey tie and a grey shirt and a grey coat with that grey suit? It's all too grey! She said I could stop hoiking up my skirt though. She said that two turns on the waistband to make it a mini was not going to achieve ostensible invisibility. Neither were over-the-knee socks that looked like stockings. Normal socks were fine, she said.

So when Sarah finally got home I told her the whole story about the fire and she said she thought it wasn't necessarily Kathryn who had done it. She said that just cos a teenager nicks stuff from small kids doesn't mean they'd set fire to things. But I said it was for definite. Sarah didn't understand then how Kathryn Cowell was behind everything at South Haringey Secondary.

From the start everyone said that the fire in the languages block was started with petrol, but at the time all the police were banging on about was that it must have been started by pupils who were smoking round the back. The teachers all said that too. I guess they know we all smoke round there so they put two and two together and made five fucking hundred. The building is right next door to the recreation ground, we call it the Rec, and all the kids that were in languages for first lesson got evacuated to the middle of the Rec, which they all thought was fucking hilarious because all the time we're told we're not allowed to go there. Half of them just walked straight out of the smoking building, straight into the Rec then straight out the other side, fag in hand, home to *Jeremy Kyle* and Marmite on toast, and the police got really annoyed because Mrs Backhouse couldn't say who was missing in the fire and who was missing at home. The point is though that James Arney, he's in Year 9, he got hurt. His legs got really badly burnt. No one else did, which everyone thought was well strange. That's when the rumours started that it was Kathryn Cowell. Then someone said that one of the firemen thought he could smell petrol and that the fire maybe started because someone had thrown petrol over the wall from the Rec and it had spread into the boys' toilets. The fire engines, like three of them, drove right across the grass in the Rec, which Clare said was totally awesome.

Two ambulances drove right over the grass too and took James Arney away as well as like five girls who'd said they'd inhaled all the smoke and couldn't stop coughing but two of them are like morons who pretend to pass out the whole time in biology practicals and the other three are cutters – you know, they slash their arms and take pills and stuff, so they were probably just in it for a bit of attention. I'm not even lying. They probably just fancied a ride in a fucking ambulance.

The fire was put out by first break but the whole of the languages block was shut down and the police weren't even allowed in cos the firemen said it was not safe and that the roof might fall in so they couldn't even investigate it. But we were all like, what's to investigate? Everyone knew it was Kathryn Cowell. After lunch we were all sent home.

No one asked the reason why Kathryn Cowell had burnt down the languages block because Kathryn Cowell doesn't do stuff for a reason. For instance it wouldn't be cos she hated languages or anything like that cos she's never been to a language lesson. Everyone thought it was probably cos she just so happened to find a can of petrol and was sitting in the Rec, where she just about lives when she isn't hanging out in the bike sheds or in the locker room, and she thought, what would be the most useful fucking thing you can do with a can of petrol when you don't have a car or a motorbike or anything? And she came up with, throw it over the fence with a match. Everyone knew that she'd get away with it.

The police interviewed her and Wino and the rest of the gang separately at the police station all afternoon, until Wino's dad, who is not known for turning up to anything much at all since he's usually inside himself, arrived just after teatime and got them all out. They each said they'd been in the locker rooms and in the town and there was no way they could've done it and the police said that until the roof was safe, they couldn't even look for any evidence. So we were all holding our breath hoping that Kathryn Cowell had left her fingerprints all over the can of petrol or something. But the way Kathryn Cowell was behaving, with her big old jaw stuck out and a fat smile on her face, we knew she hadn't.

It was dark by the time I had finished telling Sarah the whole thing. She said Kathryn would never get away with it. And I said I bet even James Arney doesn't think that. She had got a bottle of nail-varnish remover out while I talked, from the cupboard beside the sink where she keeps Paracetamols and plasters and she got some cottonwool balls from a big jar upstairs in the bathroom. She sat opposite me at the table in the lounge that Adam calls a sitting room and while I told her all about the petrol and the fire and James and Kathryn Cowell and everything, she wiped off all the crackle nail varnish and filed down my nails and put on a like plain beige nail varnish instead. I had sensible old lady's hands. I said what's wrong with my crackle nail varnish and she just shook her head and laughed and said she didn't realise it was supposed to look like that. Then she said, 'Trouble is, it takes a thief to catch a thief.' That's exactly what she said. And I was like, 'Isn't that the name of a film or something?' Cos my mum has these old video boxes on the bottom shelf in our front room and I'm sure there's one called that. And she said it was a film, yes, but also it was a kind of expression and it meant that you only really get a chance to catch bad people if you're gonna be bad yourself. And I said that was LOL coming from her, cos she never does anything wrong. And she said that it was just an idea. Afterwards, much later, she said she was only joking when she first said it but I thought it was fucking genius. It's got a fucking ring to it, right? It sounded like the sort of thing a person with plenty of fucking self-esteem would do.

27

Sarah

Day Five – 9 a.m.

'She's always so negative.'

'She's just upset, June. Like we are.'

My parents are whispering.

'I'd rather she hadn't come if she's just going to upset everyone. Going on and on at the police about that man in Sarah's room. I mean, it could have just been a mistake. Perhaps he thought he was visiting someone else. I mean, Sarah doesn't exactly look herself, does she? And I sincerely hope she doesn't start talking to the doctors again. Do you remember last time, when your mother had her bypass and Carol kept complaining that the food wasn't good enough? Went on and on at everyone. I bet she's going to go on and on.'

'How about I get you some tea?'

The door clicks open suddenly.

'Mum. Dad. This is Dr Donne. She's an expert on comas.'

My sister. Bright and breezy. There is a confusion of chair scraping. My mother is making odd sighs.

'Oh, don't get up,' *says Dr Donne – American accent. I imagine her small and dark but wide across the beam. Do you think you can tell if someone is fat by their voice?* 'No, really, there's no need.'

'Dr Donne is running a study on comas. It's a five-year study. She's getting data from all around the world.'

Wonders never cease – my sister appears to be impressed by someone.

'Um, nice to meet you, Dr Donne. I'm Brian, this is June and you've met Carol.'

'So,' *Carol, keen to get to the point,* 'can you explain to me what's going on? I know all about this intra-axial haemorrhage thing – is that what you call it? What I want to know is, what needs to happen now?'

When they had all gone, a bit later, I thought about Dr Donne's response over and over again. I didn't like what she had to say, that's true. Carol didn't like what she had to say either. But although what she said was obviously upsetting and everything, and my mother was sobbing, which didn't help, it was the way she said it that really got to me. It was simply too dramatic. She sounded too self-aware, as though she was on a stage doing Lady Macbeth or something. Maybe it's an American thing. They always seem pretty pleased with themselves, don't they? 'Have a nice day' always gets on my nerves. She seemed so impressed with herself and her knowledge, as though she knew something that we couldn't ever possibly know. She was showing off. I imagined she wore too much make-up.

'You have to prepare yourselves,' she'd said. 'In my experience of many situations similar to this one, the prognosis is very hard to come to terms with,' she'd said. 'You'll need to prepare yourselves for the fact that this may be all that's left of your sister.' That's what she said. 'This may be all that's left of your sister.' But there was a swagger in her voice. Posh, clever people get that swagger sometimes. Have you noticed? And then she said, 'You may have some difficult decisions ahead of you.' Which means flicking a switch, presumably. Thanks. I don't get a choice in this. I don't get to say how I feel. My life isn't mine. In a coma you are capable of hating someone you've never even met. I'll bet, with all her coma research, she doesn't know that.

28

Kelly

Day Five – 10 a.m.

I'm back in the hospital. I keep thinking that Sarah is just pretending to be asleep and that she's gonna suddenly sit up in bed and laugh at me and go, ha, fooled you. Once, when no one else was in here, I waved my hand in front of her face and pinched her arm to see if she would wake up. Not too hard. I didn't want to leave a fucking bruise or nothing. She didn't wake up.

They took her bandages off. She looks more normal. Well, she looks less fucking scary. The swelling on her face has gone down and although her cheeks are kind of green with bruises, and she still looks totally weird with no hair, she's actually starting to look more like her. The nurses have asked me to bring a picture in so they can see what she looks like pretty, but I haven't got any really. They've seen the wedding ones on TV. She looked really pretty there. When she had long hair. Sarah's not big on being photographed. She says she's not pretty any more. She says she doesn't mind, though.

Sarah's not the sort of person to do like random things. I mean, dangerous things. She's careful. You know, like, she wouldn't wanna go on a zip wire like we did on the Year 6 trip to that activity centre in Wales last year. And she definitely wouldn't, like, climb a rope ladder or go up one of them rock-climbing walls. Well, not for fun. But going for tea every evening before Adam got home, I got to know her quite a bit. Like I wasn't her best friend yet or nothing, but she used to tell me stuff about work and all that and although she was like totally quiet and shy and everything, she wasn't weak or stupid, even though sometimes people thought she was and treated her like she was. She'd started to play baseball with the copyediting team from her publishing company. They had team T-shirts that had printed on them 'QUIETLY JUDGING YOU', which she said was hilarious cos everyone else had things like 'THE LEGAL EAGLES' or 'THE HR FOXES'. She said she'd never felt intimidating before. She'd never played baseball before either. She said she was rubbish. It was on Wednesday lunchtimes. She got new running shoes. She made some new friends. Well, not friends exactly.

After I told her about the whole Kathryn Cowell thing, we used to talk nearly every day. I'd go round her house after she got back and we'd talk about my homework or Clare, or how my dad was like rubbish, stuff like that. But mostly we talked about Kathryn Cowell. Sarah said that Kathryn Cowell was secretly not really like the person she pretended to be. Sarah said that she was overcompensating. I don't know what she meant by that. And she'd tell me to blend in as much as I could, like the whole not-being-noticed thing. And I stopped with the ponytail and the make-up. And I stopped with the fucking up my uniform thing. And I got used to the old-lady nails. She said I could stop being Blondie now and start being Kelly again. And she told me she'd seen me a couple of months before, from her window, and how I yanked Billy and she said that behaving like that was like turning into Wino. And she said we didn't need to be bullies, we just needed to sort out how to deal with the bullies. She said that just cos they're bigger don't mean they have to win.

The nice one, Beth, she just came in and told me how to watch for signs of brain function. She says when I talk to Sarah I should see if she blinks. I should watch her fingers to see if they twitch. So I'm sitting right next to the bed on the squishy chair that Sarah's dad always falls asleep in, staring at her left hand. There's a tube going into her hand and if you look really carefully you can see the vein it's pumping into. There's blue tape and white tape holding it in place. I'm blowing on her fingers and the tiny blond hairs and the corner of the tape that isn't sticking any more move in the breeze. But her fingers don't twitch and neither do her eyes.

I realise I'm about to cry, which would be totally lame, so I go on talking to Sarah about the fire and all that shit. It was the same day that we were booked up to go to the self-defence part of our empowerment module at the community centre. The park was ribboned off by the police, but the community centre was open and although I hadn't even started my homework cos I was so fucking wired, I agreed to go just cos I thought at least it won't be all about the fire, which was all everyone else was talking about. And Sarah said she didn't have that much to do

either. We hadn't told my mum about the classes. We'd been saying that occasionally we just went up to get some chips from the
chip shop on Green Lanes cos Sarah said that was probably best.
And my mum believed her cos she's a grown-up and grown-ups
think grown-ups don't lie.

That empowerment module was one of the funniest bits of
the whole class. Module! Like we were sitting fucking GCSEs.
Most of the group, to be honest, were a bit do-goody and frankly
fucking hopeless. Some of them were way beyond fucking help.
It was all too gushy, if you ask me. It sounded more like AA than
empowerment. My dad, when I thought I had a dad, went to
AA twice a week cos my mum said she'd leave him if he didn't.
I overheard that while tracing spirals on the wallpaper in the
hall. And he went for like two years and it was all totally fine.
And then he got shit-faced one night and stole all the money out
of my mum's bank account. She got the locks changed there and
then, and that was the absolute end. She actually said, 'This is
the absolute end.' And it was.

Empowerment apparently involves understanding how to
not behave like a victim. Believe it or not, when approached by
a potential mugger, the immediate response that you give sends
out signals to the attacker of how empowered you are. Sarah
said that next time I got cornered by Wino again, or Kathryn
Cowell for that matter, for my dinner money or my mobile,
well I would DEFINITELY stand more of a chance if I sent out
empowered signals. She was joking, but the instructor wasn't.
And how do you send out empowered signals? Karate. And
during the entire hour we laughed just about the whole fucking

time. I'm not even lying. I didn't even think about the fire once, it was just too funny.

The guy was totally useless. I think he used to be one of the homeless people getting a free lunch and he saw a sign looking for a self-defence teacher. He was Moroccan. Do they even have karate in Morocco? He had a life-size plastic man mannequin with kind of big plastic wavy orange hair and red plastic trunks and a great big smile on his face, and he hung on a chain from his hair on a metal stand. Erol – that was the instructor's name, not the mannequin's – demonstrated his moves on it. And when he chopped him, the mannequin would start to swing on his chain, and his smile and his big red bum turned round and round – smile–bum–smile–bum – and it just killed us. Sarah said she had actually almost wet herself. Erol didn't appear to be able to see as far as the back of the class so was totally fucking unaware that we were bent double. LOL or what? Even Lucy with the long red hair started to shriek with laughter. He said you were supposed to yell really loud if you were jumped on, so you could draw attention to yourself to get help, plus you could unsettle your attacker. 'Arrrggghh,' he shouted. 'UNSETTLE YOUR ATTACKER,' he yelled. Then you were meant to go for these like weak areas of the body. 'STRIKE THE VITAL POINTS,' the little man screamed as he jabbed his fingers into the mannequin's eyes and Adam's apple. At which point we literally fell over. I nearly peed myself as well.

The other ladies in the class, Lucy, Shirley, other Lucy, Elisabeth and Belinda, as well as Fleur, were there, and all of them, including Fleur, which can't be fucking right since she's sposed to be in charge of the fucking group, seemed to be totally paranoid about being attacked. Every time he asked a question like 'Have you ever felt you were being followed home?' or 'Have you ever been stared at on the tube?' they shot their arms up in the air. On the back row we were wide-eyed. We wondered where all the middle-aged-women attackers had suddenly come from. Sarah said they all took life far too seriously.

Then, randomly out of nowhere, the fat blond woman Belinda shut us up. Sarah said she had a really big house, although I don't know how she knew that, and she always came to the lessons fully made up with false eyelashes and everything. For a karate lesson! Who'd do that? She slurred her words too. Sarah said she kept a bottle of vodka wrapped up in a towel in her bag. Sarah said she probably only came to get away from an overly possessive husband. I didn't really know what that meant, not at the time. Anyway, it was right at the end of the session, and all of a sudden Belinda asked from the front row, 'Excuse me,' in her slurred posh voice, she was quite posh, 'excuse me, can you tell me how to do a temple blow?' Well, Erol nearly crapped his pants. He was suddenly like sweating all over the place. He said that the temple blow was not something to be taken lightly. No. He said that he shouldn't even talk about it. No, he COULDN'T talk about it AT ALL. He mumbled and pushed the mannequin a bit so he swung some more and flashed its smile and its pants. He said it was a potentially fatal blow and not something for a self-defence class. He said, 'It's not because the skull is a bit thin at the temple – that's what most people think and they're quite, quite wrong – it's because it's flat and if you get a good enough bit of a swing at it, you could really cause some damage, if you hit it flat on.' And then he said that he'd said too much. FAR TOO MUCH. And he got even sweatier and changed the subject. Sarah said my eyebrows looked like they were going to shoot off my head. Belinda had a notepad out. I'm not even lying.

We were still laughing as we walked home past the entrance to the Rec. In the orange streetlight we could see the ribbons of plastic police tape stopping people going in the park until the police had figured out who had done the petrol. I said to Sarah that a bit of plastic tape wasn't gonna keep anyone out. And Sarah said they had CCTV in the road so if anyone went in they would get caught on film. And then when we went past the grey camera halfway up the lamp post, we saw it was hanging down on its wires and that someone had stuck a big gob of gum in the middle of the lens.

One of Kathryn's homies, no doubt. Sarah said it could have been anyone. And I said that everyone knows it's Kathryn's gang – they make a game of knocking out the camera. They stand on the back of a bike and like whack it as they go past. They keep a baseball bat stashed on the roof of the bus shelter. Just for that. The gum is their calling card. And the police don't do a thing. Fucking useless fucking police bastards.

We were just getting into the last stretch of road when Sarah asked me if I was really certain who had burnt down the languages block. And I said like, 'duh', and she said did I think Kathryn Cowell would get caught and I was like, 'as if'. And she goes maybe there would be some evidence that would put Kathryn or maybe one of her gang at the scene, and I was like,

'No way, unless she chucked her own fucking lighter over the wall.' And Sarah said, 'Maybe that's the plan then. Remember, it takes a fucking thief to catch a fucking thief?' She was really funny sometimes. Cos she never said 'fucking' so it was like really, really LOL when she did. So it was her idea you see, all along.

I said that to the nurses. That Sarah was LOL funny. Beth, she says she will be again. She keeps asking me all the time about Sarah. And now that the swelling has gone I think they feel really sorry for her. They can see she's not the type who'd ask to get her face smashed in. Not normal for Tottenham.

Beth has uncovered her toes to show me how to tickle them. Sarah's purple nail polish is starting to grow out. There are bits of bare nail where the polish has chipped off. She would totally die if she saw that. I think about trying the tickling thing when Beth has gone. I stare at her fingers. It feels like she's not there any more. She's just a body.

29

Sarah

Day Five – 11 a.m.

The man who is trying to kill me has been arrested!

That's what Lisa told Lucinda. She thinks he was trying to kill me too.

She didn't know what they charged him with.

I don't suppose it's a punishable offence to sit next to someone's bed in Critical Care. He's being questioned. They've put two men on the ward door. Policemen. I feel safe. Safer.

They're here making the bed.

'But, Lisa, did you tell the police that?'

Lucinda is whispering.

'Well, no, I didn't say that. I mean, I'm in enough trouble already, aren't I?'

'I think you should have said. I mean, what did he need to know for?'

Know what?

'Lots of people are interested in how a life-support machine works. I tell people all the time! He didn't look like a murderer. He looked kind of nice.'

'Jesus, Lisa. Your taste in men is worse than your taste in underwear.'

'What do you mean?'

'Nothing. Seriously. Nothing.'

So maybe he was trying to kill me. This is all so hard to understand. Why would someone try to kill me? What did I do?

What did I fucking do?

I've decided.

What I mean is ... I'VE DECIDED.

For some reason I can remember Adam saying that it wasn't up to me to decide anything so I may as well not bother saying, 'I've decided.' But I remember that annoyed me and I feel sure that recently I've been deciding things that don't include Adam. Anyway, I'VE DECIDED that the only thing I can do is get better. If I don't get out of here soon someone is going to switch me off. You may think I'm sounding ambitious given my circumstances. But I don't have an option, do I? So as of now I'm going to prove Doctor Doom wrong. I'm going to pull myself out of this.

I shall implement a regime. A workout. Like we do at baseball. If I do mental stretches maybe they will build the channels in my brain.

I alternate stretching with searching for memories. I'm trying to stay conscious in my head for as long as possible. No sinking.

From seeing Adam in the hat at our wedding in Southwark Register Office, I've started to remember so much more about me and about us, before we were married.

I remember school. I remember being asked to read out loud in English and being unable to get the words out. Stuttering. And asking the English teacher not to ask me again, and him understanding. I remember being frightened of this one particular teacher. Mr Johnson, he was called. He stared at me. All the time. Even in the playground he would search me out and follow me with his eyes. I remembered having piano lessons with a man who always got me to start playing and then left the room and watched me through a crack in the door. He thought I couldn't see his cheek pinched against the door frame. I could hear him breathing. I gave up the piano and my mother slapped me around the face for it. Said that I was lazy. I remembered saying nothing. Just standing there with my face stinging. No tears. No cry. And that made her slap me again.

I remember now how I first met Adam – in a bar, after an office party. Out of the corner of my eye I saw Adam beckoning me and laughing and I thought, wow, how amazing to be so confident. I remember how he talked and talked and talked. And then all the next week he would call me all the time and we'd talk for ages and as soon as I had said goodbye and put the phone down he would call me back and say he missed talking to me and then talk some more. And then he asked me out. And at first I said no. I said I didn't want a boyfriend. But he seemed different. He was so pleased with himself that he didn't need to undermine me.

I remembered our first date – well, our first proper date. We met at the tube station. And he was late. I went back into the tube station to find a map to see if I could find his road, in case I'd got it wrong and he was at home. I stared at the map for like ten minutes. And asked the man at the ticket desk. And when I went back outside he was standing waiting. And he asked me where I'd been. And he said he'd been waiting for over half an hour. I knew he hadn't. I wondered why he'd lied.

I had bought two bottles of wine because I didn't know what was good wine and what was bad wine, because I'd never really bought wine before, and I thought that if I bought two maybe one might be right. He took the bag, I thought to carry it. But he pulled the bottles out one at a time, and frowned at each one. 'Next time,' he said, 'just buy one good bottle.' I wanted to cry. Then he kissed me on my nose and laughed. He put the bottles down and picked me up in his arms and swung me around like you would a child. And then he handed me back the bag. Later, he said the wine tasted corked. I had no idea what that meant. He was much older than me, you see. He was wiser and more sophisticated. He had opinions. I didn't have any opinions. He was confident and successful. He knew everything about everything. And I felt safe.

'It's HIS brother.'

The door has opened and there's a loud whisper.

'What? Lisa, what are you going on about now?'

That's Beth.

'Lucinda said to tell you, it's HIS brother, not hers.'

'Adam's brother? Didn't they check to see if he had a brother?'

'Who?'

They are both still whispering.

'The police!'

'I don't know. I'm just telling you what Lucinda said. Apparently he's called Ash. He's saying that he never said he was her brother. Said he was her brother-IN-LAW. He didn't, though. He's a liar. I know what I heard.'

The door closes.

Brother-IN-LAW.

I don't remember any brother-in-law. Brother-in-law.

Why doesn't that make me feel any safer?

30

Kelly

I talked to Sarah for ages this morning. And that nurse. She kept asking me about Adam's brother but I really don't know anything. Not about him. Sarah never mentioned him. At least it's not Adam's fucking ghost. Beth said she doesn't think that ghosts wear parkas.

I lost it slightly. Well, this guy Ash sounds fucking weird. I mean, where's he fucking sprung from. Sitting by her bed? In the night? Fuck. What was he doing here? Any brother of Adam's has got to be fucking bad news.

The nurse parked me in the Family Room. She got me a cup of tea. With two sugar cubes. The box is holding up. Just. I had a talk with myself and told me to grow some fucking bollocks. I used to have bollocks.

Did I tell you yet how I chucked Kathryn Cowell's lighter over the other side of the wall? God, I was so fucking proud of myself then. Ask me where I got those bollocks from. Ask me where I got the fucking bollocks to go back into the school, the same night, at like ten o'clock, when actually only the cleaners are there, and unlock Kathryn Cowell's fucking locker with my identical pink padlock key, take out her fucking lighter (the one with her initials on) and then, and this was the totally freaky bit, walk back towards the Rec, like when it was literally totally dark and full of police ribbon, and chuck it over the wall. I was shitting my pants. Seriously. I was on a total mission. I guess this is what that lady Fleur was talking about when she said – now what the fuck did she say? Oh yeah, 'Be the mistress of your own destiny.' I really liked that – made me think I was a fucking superhero – but, anyway, maybe she weren't expecting that, right?

You probably think I was mad. You probably think I shouldn't interfere with the police stuff. You don't know Kathryn Cowell. You don't know what our school is fucking like. You don't know what happened to James Arney.

That totally freaked me out, when I heard about James. That's what made me do it. He had been taken to this like special burns unit thing in Cambridge. They came and got him in a helicopter from the hospital and his mum went with him in the actual helicopter. And it wasn't just the fact that the burns were so bad that upset me, it was also cos I found out from Clare that everyone was saying that Wino had done James cos he wouldn't cough up his dinner money. And then it turned out that one of Kathryn's other twat gang members, Tom Bush, had already relieved him of his dinner money when he'd arrived at school that morning in the bike sheds, which is what James had said all along but Wino didn't believe him, and Kathryn Cowell said to torch him. So they did. They'd set fire to his trousers in the boys' toilets. They'd sprayed him with lighter fluid. And he'd like fainted. It was first lesson so everyone thought he must just be away. Then they set fire to the toilets too. And then, to try to make it look like an outside job, they chucked the petrol over the wall outside the back of the toilets. And that's why the police had decided that it must have been some kind of rival gang or something. But everyone in the entire fucking school knew that it wasn't. Not that anyone would tell the police that, though, cos if you did it would be your house next.

When I'd told Sarah that I was gonna actually go and get the lighter and chuck it over the wall, she said I shouldn't do it. She said she'd been joking when she said it was a good idea and that it was far too dangerous and that my mum would kill her if she found out. But I said it was like zero risk. There'd be no one in the locker room, cos everyone had been sent home and anyway it was too late. I totally geekified my uniform – I found some proper school socks, I got the boring shoes my mum bought me at the start of the term, no more turned-up collar and Sarah had already dyed my hair back to my normal boring mouse brown. With no make-up, I looked like I was fucking seven years old or something. I said to Sarah, 'So am I invisible, then?' and she pretended she couldn't see me. She kept saying, 'Where are you, where are you?' So, while I was still giggly after our self-defence class and everything, I walked back to school. I went in through the side door by the art block, which you can unbolt from the outside, and then went down by the bike sheds next to the humanities block and into the locker room. And I never even nearly got seen by anyone. It was amazing. I walked right under the broken CCTV outside the Rec and just for a laugh I jumped up onto the bench just to see if the baseball bat was still on the roof of the bus shelter. And it was still there. Waiting. Probably covered in their prints. But the pigs don't ever bother to look up there. It's way too much trouble. Requires way too much thinking, looking up. I kept in the shadows of the hedges and garden walls, avoiding the streetlights, like she said, with my head down – not too far down cos that's weird, just down enough not to meet anyone's eye. People look at pretty people, she said. Stare at them. People don't like pretty people because they're pretty, so they stare. People are attracted to blond hair. Glittery lip gloss in Pepto-Bismol pink. Better to not be pretty, then. Better not to be noticed. I didn't see anyone. And no one saw me.

Afterwards I went straight back to Sarah's because I was way excited. I was so hot and buzzing. Sarah's car wasn't there so I figured she must have just gone somewhere cos she always parked right outside. So I just sat on her doorstep and waited. And got my breathing back to normal. I just needed to be quiet for a bit. And then a door opened inside the house, and I heard Adam's voice. And I was just about to leave because I never go in when Adam is there, when I heard Sarah as well, although she was talking really quietly. And he said, and I remember it word for word, he said, 'You're a fucking whore. Pretending to go to the chip shop with the next-door neighbour's little girl. What were you doing? Looking out for men to fuck? What are you?' and she didn't answer. So he repeated it, he said, 'You're a fucking whore, Sarah. What are you?' And there was a bang, like a thud, followed by a cry. And then Sarah said in a fucking weird fucking small voice, 'I'm a fucking whore.' And I have never been so scared in my entire fucking life. That's what Adam was like. I bet his fucking brother is too.

31

Sarah

Day Six – 9 a.m.

'Morning, Sarah.'

Morning, Beth.

'Morning, Mrs Beresford.'

Morning, Mother.

'Is Mr Malin in today, do you know at all? My daughter wants to see him.'

'Your daughter?'

More drama?

'My other daughter, Carol. Didn't you meet her yesterday?'

'No, I don't think I did. I can check for you. Would you like some tea? I think they are doing the rounds.'

'Brian is getting it, actually. But thank you.'

The door opens.

'Morning, Mother.'

Here she is.

'Hello, love. Did you sleep well?'

'No, Mother, of course I didn't sleep well. That Travelodge is a shithole.'

'Your father finds it very pleasant. It's the buffet breakfast.'

'I might go and stay at Sarah's.'

There go my clothes.

'Do you think you should? It's such a rough area. I always told her it was rough.'

'Maybe the thought of me rifling through her clothes will wake her up. WAKE UP, SARAH. THAT PURPLE VELVET SCARF IS ALL MINE.'

She is quite funny at times. You can have my scarf, just get me out of here.

'Have the police found out what they were doing in White Hart Lane yet? Maybe I could find a diary or something. Has anyone looked on her laptop?'

'Brenda – you know, the next-door neighbour – told the police that she was at the community centre.'

'The community centre? What for?'

The community centre in the park. I remember. That's the place I used to go to with Kelly, I think.

'Sarah was seeing a mediation counsellor.'

'A what?'

'It's some kind of therapy for couples.'

I'm quite sure I didn't. Doesn't sound like me at all.

'That's what Brenda said. I can't imagine my daughter going in for some kind of counselling, can you?'

'You mean you can't imagine your daughter's husband going in for some kind of counselling. What *could* a counsellor tell

Adam, do you think? He was the world fucking expert on everything.'

'The police think they must have been having difficulties.'

'What kind of difficulties? Why doesn't anyone ever say what they mean? Perhaps Adam's brother can tell us. He's coming in today. Ashley.'

What? Don't let him near me. Don't let him in. LISTEN TO ME. DO NOT LET HIM IN!

'What do you mean? Didn't you say he was under arrest?'

'They let him go. He had nothing to do with it. Total alibi. He was landing at the airport when the mugging happened. Arrived at Sarah's house and it was pitch black. Someone told him that they'd been brought up here after the accident. It was late.'

HE'S A LIAR.

'Well, he's been hanging around here enough. He's not welcome, is he, Brian? Where's he gone now?'

HE WILL TRY TO KILL ME.

'Langlands called me to say that they'd let him out and that he wanted to come in. He tried you and Dad but you didn't pick up. What could I say?'

'Here's your father – didn't they have the biscuits, Brian?'

'No, June. No biscuits. I can go to the vending machine. They have muesli bars.'

'Dad, what did the police say about the mediation counselling?'

'I'm not sure about muesli bars. I don't really care for them. They hurt my gums.'

'Carol, I have no idea, you'll have to ask your mother. Do you want a muesli bar or not, June? June?'

'Brian, was it cranberry or plain?'

I love the fact that the muesli bar is taking on a life of its own.

'I don't think there's any point in you getting upset about Sarah seeing a counsellor, Carol. No, thank you, Brian.'

'I'll have a muesli bar, Dad. I'm not getting upset. I'm just wondering why the police want to know. What can that possibly have to do with anything?'

'It's a murder case, Carol, that's why.'

Since when?

'No, it is not, Dad. Murder means it was planned. It was a mugging that went wrong. Unlawful killing is what they said.'

'The police are only doing their job, Carol.'

'I can quite see that someone might have liked to murder Adam. I myself could have done it a number of times. But no one would do anything to Sarah. She was a mouse. A sweet, quiet, dull little mouse.'

'She was not dull.'

Thank you, Dad.

'Can you not talk about her as though she's not here? What are you playing at, Carol? Did you just come here to cause trouble?'

That's my dad. Angry suits him.

'She just lacked confidence, Brian, didn't she? That's all. She was such a happy child. I don't know what happened. Do you remember, Brian? When she won that medal for Irish dancing? When she played a donkey in the school nativity?'

I remember James Stock. He sat on me and ripped my dress open.

'What about when she cut all her hair off.'

'That was when she was older.'

'She was what, seven? Eight? Why did she do that?'

'Carol. Can you stop? You aren't helping.'

'Why does any child do something naughty? You'll have to ask her. If she ever bothers to wake up.'

'June! Can you not speak like that? What are you thinking?'

'She hacked it off, Carol, since you ask. She looked like she belonged in a workhouse.' 'What about when she broke her ankle? And didn't tell you.'

'What do you mean?'

'She didn't tell you that she had broken her ankle. You didn't take her to hospital for three days. What kind of child wanders around with a broken ankle without telling anyone about it? A quiet, dull one.'

The door is opening again.

'Hello, Mr and Mrs Beresford.'

'Oh, hello, Mr Malin. This is my daughter Carol.'

'I'm sorry for the sad circumstances, Carol.'

'Oh, you're Mr Malin. I get to meet you, at last! I wanted to talk to you, as we seem to have some differing opinions here about the prognosis of my sister.'

'Yes, I heard that you spoke to my colleague, Dr Donne. I'm sorry about that. We don't always share the same views over intra-axial haemorrhages.'

'And what is your view then, Mr Malin?'

'I'm sure we can talk about that at some point, Carol, but right now I need to talk to your parents about Sarah's medical history.'

'What about it?'

'Mrs Beresford, what do you know about previous injuries that Sarah might have suffered?'

'Why, she's always been very healthy, doctor. Not really anything to speak of, I don't think. Brian?'

'What about her ankle? We were just talking about that, weren't we, Mother?'

'Well, yes, there's her ankle. That was when she was eight. She fell off –'

'I'm talking about more recent injuries. It appears that your daughter has had some significant injuries over the last three years. She has had … um, a broken arm, three broken fingers, a fractured patella, a broken leg, a dislocated shoulder and a serious cranial fracture.'

'No, I don't think so, doctor. That can't be right.'

'I'm not asking you, Mrs Beresford. I'm telling you.'

'There must be some kind of mistake.'

'No, no kind of mistake. We have had her records sent over to us and it seems she was quite the regular at the Royal Free Hospital in Hampstead.'

'That's near where she used to live.'

'A regular?'

'A regular patient. She was regularly "accident prone".'

'What are you trying to say, doctor? That she did this to herself?'

'No, I'm not, Miss Beresford. I'm saying that for someone to have sustained that many injuries over two years, we would normally expect some kind of difficulty at home.'

'Difficulty?'

My mother is starting to cry again.

'What does "difficulty" actually mean, doctor? We keep on hearing it.'

That was my dad.

'He means that Adam was doing it.'

Don't be ridiculous.

'Adam was doing what?'

'Beating her up. Is that it, doctor?'

'The incidence of the injuries, and the cranial fracture in particular, is frankly concerning.'

'Because?'

'Because, Carol, that's the reason she is in a coma now. That cranial fracture gave her skull a weakness that meant that she was predisposed to brain trauma. Any fall, even a mild one, could have caused a considerable problem. We wouldn't have expected an intra-axial haemorrhage necessarily. No one could. That is surprising. But the brain is complicated. Full of surprises. However, she will have been made aware of her condition. She would certainly have been told to avoid situations where she could possibly hit her head.'

'So it's her own fault that she got pushed over, is it? She should have avoided going out at night just in case a mugger pushed her? God, this place sucks.'

I didn't know. I don't know anything.

'Plus it puts a different light on the investigation.'

'In what way exactly, Mr Malin?'

'It means that the force with which she hit the pavement may have been much lighter than we previously thought. It means that in her case the trauma may actually have been an accident. She had no other injuries. Even the facial bruising was caused by the brain trauma.'

'It doesn't really make any difference to us right now, though, does it? She's still in a fucking coma.'

'It will make a difference to the muggers, though. The difference between five years and life imprisonment.'

'Well, big deal, Mr Malin. Big deal. Come back when you have something positive to tell me about my sister, rather than helping the muggers get off.'

'I apologise if you think that's my only interest. I would have thought that it would be of concern to all of you that your sister, your daughter, was being subjected to domestic abuse.'

'We only have your word for that.'

'No, Carol. We have medical records as long as my arm.'

The door opens and closes.

'Who's rewriting history now then, Mother?'

'Well, I don't believe a word of it. They have obviously got the wrong person. Haven't they, Brian?'

'I told you she was a victim. Fuck. Why didn't she tell me? Fuck.'

'We would have known if he was being violent. She would have said. Brian. She would have said, wouldn't she? Brian! Where are you going now?'

The door slammed. When they'd all stopped arguing, when they'd all gone, the sound went completely again. The darkness got darker. I strained to hear anything but there was nothing there.

And now, in my mind, all I can see is the outline of Adam, bent double, leaning on a lamp post, vomiting onto the pavement. Somehow it was easier having no memory, being no one.

32

Kelly

I came in early this morning to see Sarah. I sat with her for a bit until her parents came. I heard them coming and slipped out without talking to them. Down to the Family Room. They don't come in here. They don't like the mugs, apparently. I don't like the fucking mugs either.

The day after I chucked the lighter over the wall – the day after the fire – I didn't feel like going to see Sarah at her house. I didn't go the next day either. School was on half-days cos the languages block was still dangerous, which was obvs totally brilliant. I went down Wood Green with Clare and everyone. I couldn't decide if I didn't wanna go round Sarah's cos I thought she would be hurt and I couldn't bear that, and also because I thought she was gonna lie to me. I also couldn't work out why I was so fucking angry, not just with Adam, who I'd always thought was a total prick, but with Sarah too. I think

I was confused by all this shit about self-confidence and sticking up for yourself and being comfortable in your own skin, and then there she was letting a fucking monster beat her up.

I didn't stay mad at her for long, though. I didn't see her again for a week or two, until the weekend when she was coming back from somewhere in her car, and I was going to TK Maxx to meet Clare. It was totally awks. Adam was watching from the window. I saw him when I was locking the door. I think I was pretending to be in a hurry. She had a fucking enormous bruise that she was trying to hide under her sunglasses. As we walked past each other, I said, like really quietly, 'What the fuck happened to your eye?' and she kind of whispered, 'Did you do the lighter?' but we both said it at the same time so neither of us really heard what the other one said. We burst out laughing. And she said we really wouldn't make very good secret agents.

That nurse, Beth, she says the police have found out about Adam's brother now. He's been living somewhere else. You know. Not in England. He's only been here for like a month. When Langlands asked him what his occupation was, he said he was a businessman. Langlands asked him what that meant. He told Beth he's well dodge. They've also found out about Adam. I thought they would. I actually thought that they would've done a dig around like straight after it happened. I mean, someone gets killed, you'd have thought they would have checked to see if they had a record, wouldn't you? He'd almost got done for GBH. But they let him off. Not enough evidence in the end, or something. Sarah didn't even find out about it until, what, six months ago? My mum says Sarah's medical records have given Adam away to the police. Malin wanted to check something out about the old fracture they'd found on the MRI scan and got this entire fucking report of accidents and stuff from her doctor. It said she'd like tripped on the stairs, slipped in the bath, fallen off a stepladder, apparently. That's apparently with a capital A. You wouldn't believe the number of fucking accidents that can happen to one person in like two years. And neither did Malin, and neither did the police.

'Mrs McCarthy,' says Detective Inspector Langlands. He's back in the Family Room. He's actually sat in the same chair the drug smuggler was in. My mum has her back to him making tea. 'Mrs McCarthy, regarding the list of injuries that has been supplied by the patient's general practitioner ...' Why do these people always complicate things? Why don't they just say whatever the fuck they want to know? My mum is dunking a teabag up and down in the mug. 'It seems that the patient, um, Sarah, had undergone significant and diverse trauma over the course of the past two years and whilst it seems relatively possible that Sarah's parents – Sarah's family –' he corrects himself, 'who don't live in the direct vicinity, may not have been made aware of the injuries, it is rather harder to suppose that someone living, say, next door to the victim would fail to notice, let's say, for the sake of argument, a broken leg, Mrs McCarthy. Do you see my point?'

My mum has her mug of tea and is putting like a ton of sugar in, which is what she does when she secretly wants a port and lemon or a fat G&T.

'Detective Inspector,' she starts, with a sigh, which means she's about to diss him. 'I don't know every single thing that may or may not have happened in Sarah and Adam's house, despite them living, as you say, next door. I also don't know every single thing that may or may not have happened in my other neighbour's house either, the one who lives on the other side. In fact, I don't even know the name of my neighbour who lives on the other side. And do you know why, Detective Inspector? Do you know why?' (She's getting a bit shrill now.) 'Because I do not live *in* my neighbours' houses, I live in *my* house. Do you know what goes in your neighbours' houses, Detective Inspector? I don't suppose you do, any more than I do.'

The Detective Inspector looks bloody furious. I'm pretending not to look through the glass from the corridor. I'm pretending I can't hear anything.

'Forgive me for pointing out the blindingly bleeding obvious, Mrs McCarthy, but you wouldn't have to live in the same house as someone to spot a thigh-to-ankle leg brace, now, would you?' he says, with a fat sneer on his face.

'And on another point . . . I have been given reason to believe that Sarah was seeing a mediation counsellor at the community centre. Would you happen to know if *that* is correct, Mrs McCarthy?'

'Again, Detective Inspector,' my mum replies, gulping her tea and leaving a pink stain on the rim of the Arsenal mug, 'I have better things to do with my time than standing around all day behind my net curtains in the hope that I see my neighbours' comings and goings. Perhaps,' she says with a broad smile, 'you don't.'

I know why my mum is lying. She doesn't like the police. Actually, she really fucking hates the police. And she particularly really fucking hates Langlands. She literally drove Sarah to Casualty, twice, and like rang for the ambulance and everything the time she found Sarah unconscious at the bottom of her stairs. But she doesn't see the point of the police, you see. She's not disrespectful or nothing. She just doesn't see what they can do. Specially after what happened with my dad. After she threw him out for stealing all the money, and he kept coming round. Kept asking to see her. Kept telling her that he missed her. Calling through the letterbox. Even after she'd thrown him out. So she called the police. And when the pigs arrived, they just beat him up. He was pissed, admittedly. But they broke his fucking ribs. Two of 'em. One minute my mum was inside trying to stop him getting inside the house. And the next minute he was lying outside on the pavement and she was trying to stop them kicking his head in. He's never been back since. Never. Never will.

Langlands is still banging on about the mediation. How is my mum sposed to know about that? Why doesn't he just go and ask the fucking counsellor? What a total prick. I'm pretty sure she would tell him, actually. I know it's sposed to be like private and everything, but Adam got seriously fucked at the first appointment. He did a Special Brew special. Said there was no point in him being there. Said Sarah had no right to trick him into coming. Said there was nothing wrong with their marriage. And said that he wanted to kill her. There and then. That he was actually going to kill her. So they banned him. Hilarious. Banned from attending his own fucking mediation class. From then on they locked all the doors as soon as she was in. I think more for their own sakes than for hers, but never mind. And you know what, he waited outside for her every week. Every fucking week. Nine o'clock. By the bus shelter. With his can of Special Brew in one hand and a Marlboro Red in the other. And, according to Sarah, the mediation counsellor told her that she was never really sure that Sarah was going to make it back the following week.

My mum doesn't know any of that, though. But she wouldn't tell Langlands nothing even if she did.

I will wait another ten minutes and then if they don't stop I'm gonna get the bus home. Mum's still jabbering on about me going back to school, but I already told her Wednesday is just homework anyway. May as well do it at home. In front of *Pointless*.

I hear the buzzer go and there's a few seconds before anyone comes in. The old geezer is standing there, looking expectant. When whoever it is comes through the door the old man starts to look doubtful. I'm craning my neck to see but I don't wanna be too fucking obvious, do I?

'Check my name, old boy! I'm on your list today alright. Mr Langlands said so. Detective Inspector Bruce Langlands, I believe he's called.'

The old guy is searching. And then he nods to himself.

'And your name is?' he says.

'Ashley Weston,' he says. 'Mr Ashley Weston. You want me to spell that, old man?'

Adam's brother. What the fuck is he doing here?

'Nooo nooo. I've got your name right here, lad,' he says, and ticks his form.

I'm still craning my neck when he walks right past the door. Right past me. And he looks straight in my face. Like bold as fucking brass. Like I was scum. And he is like Adam's twin. It's like totally weird. I'm not even lying.

Then I hear June coming down the corridor too. Shouting at Brian as usual.

'Hi, you must be Carol,' he says.

Then Carol goes, 'Oh, Ash. Yes, we spoke on the phone. Thanks so much for coming.'

'Not the first time you've been either, is it, young man?' says Brian.

'Gosh, so sorry for the confusion. I just really wanted to make sure that Sarah was OK. I was just in shock, really.'

'Sorry about Adam, Ash,' says Carol, quietly. Like she's being fucking sympathetic.

'Yeah, we was close, you know?' No, they fucking weren't. What's he lying for?

And then I can't hear what they are saying cos they've walked back up the sodding hall.

What the fuck does he want? Sarah, you'd better fucking wake up fast.

33

Sarah

Day Six – 2 p.m.

'How's our patient doing today?'

That's Mr Malin.

'Isn't it your job to tell us that?'

And that's my sister.

'Hmm, yes, of course. We've been testing Sarah's vestibulo-ocular reflex today.'

'Which is ... ?'

'We inject water into the ear.'

'Gosh, how very technical, syringing her ears.'

'It *is* actually very technical. We monitor the eye movements to see if they deviate towards the ear with the water in. If they do then the brain stem is functioning normally but consciousness is impaired. If they move the opposite way it also suggests some brain function.'

'So, then, what happened with Sarah?'

'Nothing, I'm afraid.'

Terrific.

'Can we actually cut the crap, doctor? I'm so fed up of all this medical talk. Can you just tell me when she is going to wake the fuck up?'

He sighs. They're obviously getting pissed off with her.

'Consciousness is made up of two elements – awareness and wakefulness. At the moment you are awake and aware. Your sister is neither. What we've been waiting for with Sarah is to see if she finds her way back to us. What sometimes happens after a few days is that the brain function shuts down all together – that's called being brain dead. Sometimes there is wakefulness but no awareness – that's known as being in a vegetative state. From a vegetative state a patient may become minimally conscious with some awareness and eventually regain full consciousness. Very occasionally a person might get what's known as locked-in syndrome – where they are wakeful and aware but unable to move or speak.'

'Which one is Sarah?'

'We believe your sister may have suffered trauma to the brain stem. We're not sure.'

'And … ?'

'The outcome isn't good.'

'But you said that she *could* be locked in. She could be able to hear us.'

'It's not likely, though. We can do more tests and see what happens.'

'And what if she doesn't respond? Does she just stay here for ever?

'She will be able to go to a care home and remain on life support until such a time as you all choose to discontinue that. That's up to you and your parents to decide.'

He's talking really quietly. Slowly. Carefully.

'What does that mean? Can you just say what you mean?'

'If Sarah goes into a hospice you may think that removing her feeding tubes and turning off the life support is the kindest thing, in the circumstances. You will all be there for her. You can say goodbye. It can be a very moving –'

'Go to hell, Mr Malin. Go to hell.'

The door has slammed. Carol has gone. Except for the hum and bleep of the machines it is silent.

'Sarah. I don't know if you can hear me or not.'

Malin is still here.

'If you can hear me, I appreciate that you are feeling pretty scared right now, and I just want to explain to you that no one has given up on you. We are all here to try to help you get better. But *you* really are going to have to work really hard to help yourself get better too. When you first arrived on this ward we put you into what is called an induced coma – that is, we were keeping you in an unconscious state in order that we give your brain a chance to recover itself. By now, though, we have significantly reduced the intake of drugs and you should have been able to start trying to reboot your brain. I think you will understand what I mean by that. You need to remember how to open your eyes, how to move your limbs. If you concentrate really hard you will be able to do that, Sarah. And we are here watching and waiting for you to wake up. I think you can do it, Sarah. We are all right here for you.'

Crap.

Now all I want to do is cry.

I'm trying, Mr Malin. I'm trying with every sinew of my body to get my hand to move. Nothing happens. I try to feel with my fingers. Feel a sheet perhaps, a cool smooth cotton sheet under my fingers. If I try to open my eyelids, just a millimetre, I might see my dad. Or the nurses. Or Kelly. If I just try really hard I could get back. But nothing happens. I feel nothing.

I've lost myself.

Dark.

Down.

Despair.

Screaming.

And then the tapping begins.

Tap, tap-tap, tap. Tap, tap-tap, tap.

'Sarrrrrraaaahhhh. Wake up, little girl. I need my fucking money. Where is it?'

Sarrrrrrraaaahhhhh.

Tap, tap-tap, tap.

34

Kelly

Day Six – 6 p.m.

I'm parked in Sarah's room and I'm not fucking moving. That
weirdo Ash was in here earlier. He waited until they'd all gone off
then he snuck back. I fucking saw him do it. So I came in. And
I was like, 'What you looking at?' And he was like, 'A right
bolshie little kid is what. Get the fuck out of here.' And I was like,
'The nurses told me to come in so I'm staying.' And he started
coming over in a like threatening way. You know, like he was
hard. And I was about to square up to him and all that but then
I thought if he's anything like Adam he will just punch me in the
face. I'm not even lying. So I went and got Beth. And she went
in there and told him it was time to leave. I think she knows he's
up to something. And when he left I was like, 'Byyeee.' And I
waved. And he said, 'Lovely to see you, nurse', and he gave her
a big old smile. And he sort of sauntered down the corridor as
slow as you like. And Beth said he was a twat, which was funny.
And she said that I had bigger balls than him. And I told her I

learned what to do about bullies in my self-esteem classes. The ones I did with Sarah. I never told anyone at school I was going. They'd have thought I was weird. I only told Clare and she said it was like a total loser thing to do. But that was around the time that she was getting pissed off with me anyway because of Sarah and all that stuff about my hair. Our hair.

Sarah said even if I was much younger than everyone else it was still worth going and she knew this boy who was still at school and who was being bullied and he had been, not to that exact one but something nearly the same, and he had said it was definitely worth going. When I look back now, though, I realise that Sarah actually wanted to go for herself, not just for me. When we first went I thought *she* was like the odd one out. I thought everyone would be thinking 'what's she doing here?' cos she's pretty and really good at her job and everything. I thought she was just trying to get me to go. She definitely doesn't look the type who needs to stand about in a community centre writing positive thoughts on a fucking wipe board. After a while, though, especially after that trouble with Adam, I began to see that all of us there, we were just a bunch of broken things. Sarah said that was the whole point.

So what was weird ended up being what we did just about every week for like ages. Every Thursday. Seven p.m. They didn't do it in the school holidays, though, which is fucking mental cos that's when I have like nothing to do apart from all the stuff that my mum totally invents like cleaning the windows or jet-washing the crazy paving. I would have actually quite liked somewhere to go other than TK Maxx or Burger

King. We did a different topic every half-term, so like we did stuff about strengths and weaknesses. That one was actually really boring – you had to write loads of lists, like nice things people had said to you, and then you had to read them out in front of everyone, which would have been embarrassing if it weren't for the fact that half of what they all wrote was fucking insane. Like the most stupid shit I ever heard. Seriously. I was like, OMG, what the fuck is wrong with you? One woman, Shirley, she lives right opposite the sandpit in Clissold Park, she said that her mum didn't used to give her a kiss goodnight and however much she used to cry and cry, her mum wouldn't come to give her the kiss goodnight. She's like forty-two or something. You gotta be over that by forty-two, right? I actually wish my mum WOULDN'T kiss me. We did another thing called 'setting realistic expectations' and Elisabeth, who's like sixty-five and retired, she said she'd like to be a millionaire by the end of the year. And everyone just sat there and groaned, cos how's she gonna do that in like five months? And Fleur said that that wasn't really a realistic (she did that funny scratching-the-air thing with her fingers when she said 'realistic') expectation, now, was it? But she said it in a kind way and Elisabeth sucked it up. Then we did 'setting aside perfection' which was totally fucking hilarious cos Sarah is such a head case when it comes to perfection. She lines up tins in her cupboards – like tins of tomatoes and baked beans and stuff all in a row facing the same direction. She irons her knickers. She irons Adam's pants. And her tea towels. She combs her eyebrows with like a little comb and this eyebrow gel. Seriously there is gel made for eyebrows. So she was terrible at that one. She said it was cos Adam is a Virgo. Fleur said it wasn't about Adam and Sarah blushed. I'd never seen her blush before.

Then we did this half-term module on trust. Like how you should trust people and what happens if you don't have friends who you can trust and how it's all down to you and not really down to them. The best fun we had was this thing called a trust fall. Have you heard of it? It's a bit like stage diving, but without the stage. You know, you stand with your back to everyone and you kind of fold your arms in front of you and then you just fall backwards and your friends are sposed to catch you. And the idea was that you prove that you trust your friends, and if you don't trust your friends then you won't do it. And I did it straight away even though Lucy was there, the one with the long red hair, the one that's afraid all the time and I thought well she's gonna be too afraid to catch me for fear of catching something herself so I can't really fucking rely on her. But Sarah said I was small and not difficult to catch so I would be fine. But she wouldn't do it cos she was too tall and what if she was too heavy or long or everyone missed her? And she said that she'd had an injury and that if she smacked her head then she might get really ill. But no one believed that. It sounded like a totally lame excuse. So then it became a bit of a thing and every week Fleur would say, 'C'mon now, Sarah, time to do your trust fall.' And Sarah couldn't. She'd get us all in a tight group behind her and she'd fold her arms and then look over her shoulder and go, 'No. No. I can't', and run off. Fleur said she'd do it in time.

We did that self-defence thing I told you about, when the mad woman Belinda scared the shit out of the total loser Moroccan instructor. And we did this thing one time, with an orange. FML it was funny. You had to sit cross-legged on the floor and roll the orange to each other and then say a word – like any word that came into your head but you weren't sposed to think about it too hard cos that meant you weren't doing it right. Fleur said it was called word association or something. We never actually made it to the words bit, though, cos these women were so fucking bad at rolling the fucking orange. Seriously. They would like roll it into like fucking nowhere. It was like they couldn't think and roll at the same time. So Fleur would go like, 'loneliness' and roll the orange to Elisabeth and she would, at the last possible second, stop the orange and then whizz it off into like a totally random corner of the hall, staring after it like she hadn't done it, like the orange had gone off on its fucking own, and she wouldn't remember to say a word anyway. I started off trying to be helpful, going to get the orange cos half of them had taken half an hour to get onto the floor and were gonna take even fucking longer to get up again – so each time the orange shot off, I'd go and get it, sit in the circle on the floor again, roll the fucking orange again to Belinda or Lucy or Elisabeth again just for them to shoot it off into the corner while they searched their fucking empty heads for a fucking word. That was when we started giggling. We laughed so much, me and Sarah, that in the end we were sending the fucking orange all over the place too. We were rolling around on the carpet crying, it was so funny. And then everyone was. And on the way home, Sarah said that that was probably the whole point. Cos next time we went, everybody was still laughing about it, and it was like we were all suddenly really good friends.

Looking at Sarah now in the hospital bed, she doesn't look like the same person as the one who was rolling the orange, although she looks better than she did when I first saw her lying here. Her shaved head is not so fucking brutal. Her bruised face is less purple, more green.

Sarah changed, though – before the accident, I mean. Adam changed her. She never laughed so much any more. She'd got thin and quiet and her face got this sad look. And the short hair made her look older. Like an old lady, Adam said. I think the only time I saw her laugh was when we were in the community centre with our lavender ladies – that was what Sarah called them – ladies who had let purple go to their heads and had become slightly mad. She did do the trust fall. Did I tell you that? She did it on the last day of that term. Fleur said it was her last chance and that if she didn't do it we would have to all repeat the whole topic next half-term. So we all started shouting and clapping and stamping our feet going, 'Sarah! Sarah! Sarah!' We all got into position and she folded her arms, and she looked over her shoulder and wouldn't do it, and then just when we were all about to give up, she looked at us and then she smiled and then she opened her arms out like really wide, which you're not supposed to do at all, and she tipped backwards and we all caught her and we all laughed so much that we all fell over. And then we broke up for the Easter holidays.

So we didn't see anyone for a month. Sarah said that if there was a most improved badge she'd have got it that term for her trust fall.

They're taking Sarah for another brain scan this afternoon. They've reduced her medication again. I think they're getting a bit desperate. We've got to bring some music in that she likes. I'm gonna bring in a mix tape and my headphones. I'm gonna bring her back to normal with like Coldplay. I can't fucking stand Coldplay.

35

Sarah

Day Seven – 9 a.m.

'Did you hear the tox reports are back on the husband?'

Why isn't anyone saying anything about Ashley? What tox reports?

'Do you know where the square swabs are?'

'They're in the cabinet. Seems like he was fucked. Very fucked.'

Do they mean Adam was drunk?

'They've only just discovered that now?'

'I think the results got mislaid or something. Anyway, he'd sunk enough to take down a giant.'

'He was a giant.'

'No, I mean that they were shocked that anyone could have drunk that much and still be standing.'

'Do either of you know when Bed 9 is due?'

'No, Jen, sorry.'

'Ask Lisa. She's at the nurses' station. She took the call.'

'Doesn't sound like he was standing for long.'

'According to that girl, Sarah had been at a counselling session in the –'

'What, the neighbour's daughter? Kelly? How does *she* know?'

'Dunno. The police are going to investigate at the community centre – right where it happened. They want to talk to the parents again. It seems a shame. They should just leave them alone. What are they going to know about that? They've got enough to contend with.'

'Yeah, one daughter in hell and the other one from hell.'

'How very fucking true.'

What about Ash? What if he comes back?

'What's true?'

'Hi, Lisa. Is Bed 9 coming in?'

'On its way. Sarah's neighbour is here again. The one with the daughter.'

'Oh, nice. OK. She's all set. Her visitors may enter. Ta daaa.'

'Hello, Mrs McCarthy, how are you?'

Brenda.

'I'm well, Beth, thank you. How's Sarah today?'

'She's just about to open her eyes and say good morning, aren't you, Sarah?'

Sure am. I wish. I'm trying though. I'm imagining I can see. Pretending that I want to pick something up and telling my brain to go ahead and do it.

'I've brought some music in. Like that doctor said. It's Take That. Do you think that's alright? Kelly's at school, but she said Sarah wouldn't like it. Her exact words were "OMG, don't play her Take That. It'll send her over the edge." Actually she said, "It'll take her over the fucking edge", but we don't need to tell everyone that, do we? I don't know what young people listen to these days. Kelly's put some tracks on her iPod.'

'I'm sure she'll like whatever you've brought, Mrs McCarthy. Now, I've got a patient coming into Bed 9. Can you look after things here?'

Brenda. Watch me. I'm trying to open my eyes. Brenda!

'Should I be doing anything, nurse?'

'No, you're fine, dear. Just play some music and watch out to see if Sarah responds. Watch her eyes. Watch her hands. Mum and Dad are here somewhere. I think they're with the police again. But they'll be here soon.'

The door closes. Brenda is humming. Brenda. I'm here. Come near me. Watch me closely. I'm trying to open my eyes. Watch. Are they moving? Are they? Now? Are they moving?

'This CD player doesn't fucking work!'

She's talking to herself! Brenda! Watch me. Watch!

'I don't fucking believe it! Jesus, Mary and Joseph, what the fuck is wrong with this?'

Brenda. For heaven's sake!

'Would you believe it? Jesus Christ. Jesus Christ! Jesus Christ, my language! What would Father O'Shea say?'

I can feel my hands. I can! I can actually feel where my hands are! I don't believe it. I'm coming back. I'm waking up! There's a clicking and a humming sound. A CD is being ejected from a CD player. Where on earth would they have found a CD player? Brenda! Can you see my hands? I can feel my hands.

'Nurse? Nurse?'

Brenda! Don't leave now. Brenda!

'Nurse. Can you come? Nurse. This CD player isn't working.'

'Just a minute, Mrs McCarthy. We'll be there in one second.'

'But, nurse. I think it's broken. It's not going round.'

Brenda. I can feel my hands!

'Oh, hello, Mrs Beresford. Mr Beresford. Are you OK? You look upset. Is everything OK?'

Dad. Dad! Are you there? Can you hear me? Watch, I can move my hands! Someone's crying.

'Oh dear. Oh dear, Mrs Beresford. Have you had some tea? Would you like some tea? Come along. Let's get you some tea, shall we? Come along.

Dad? Brenda? Where's my mother? What's wrong? Where's everyone gone? I can feel my hands. Look!

And then the sound goes. Everything stops.

There is nothing.

I am lost.

I have disappeared.

This isn't happening.

36

Kelly

Day Seven – 7 p.m.

My mum went to see Sarah today. Sarah's mum was there crying. And her dad. The doctors have run more tests. There isn't any good news. They said she's in a 'vegetable state'. What a fucking thing to say! Harsh. Ash hasn't been back, though. Only good bit of news.

She took a Take That CD. My mum. Fuck my life, who would do that? If you were in a coma and all you could hear was fucking Gary Barlow, how crap would that be? I'd prefer being un-fucking-conscious.

My mum says I shouldn't joke about the sick. I said I'm not fucking joking. Seriously. But, anyway, she couldn't get the CD thing to work, so tomorrow I'm gonna take my iPod mini in. I'm loading it now with her Coldplay tracks even though they make my fucking teeth itch. It's the one Sarah gave me for my fourteenth birthday. It's like neon yellow. And when she gave it me she made me promise never to take it out of the house cos she said the whole idea wasn't to contribute to Kathryn Cowell's habit. That's how she said it. Whole idea. She always says 'whole idea'. And 'contribute'. She says Kathryn's a typical addict. She says you can tell an addict cos their ego is like sky high and their self-esteem is like through the floor and the gap in between is what gets filled up with addiction – whether that's drugs or alcohol or bullying. And I think that's pretty fucking smart of her, really. Once you see scum for what it is, it doesn't seem so scary.

But saying that, after they found Kathryn Cowell's lighter behind the burnt-out languages block I had got even more scared of Kathryn Cowell, even with Sarah's clever explanations. I was like literally terrified. While everyone else was like laughing their fucking heads off that Kathryn Cowell had been stupid enough to leave behind her lighter and they were all going like, 'What a total spaz', I was crapping myself. I was going, 'Oh yeah, what a total spaz', and thinking, 'I am so fucking dead.' They were taken back into the police station for another whole day; Kathryn Cowell, Wino, Alex Hall, Tom Bush and Rob Long were all interviewed again but, because they are all kids, the police are powerless. That's what my mum says. Powerless. My mum says, just you wait till they are eighteen. But that's too late for us lot at school. Sarah says we are all traumatised. She says even the teachers are traumatised. Sarah said in the end it takes a thief to catch a thief. I asked my mum what that was and she said it was a totally ancient film, so I didn't really get what Sarah was going on about then. We were talking about everything on the way to the community centre and we'd just seen Wino and, honestly, he looked like a fucking crack head. He was falling all over the place and it was only like six thirty in the evening. But even though he was shit-faced, he still looked like he was up to something, like he had a plan, on a mission, out to get someone for something. Me, probably. I said that to Sarah and she said I was over-thinking everything. And she said that now I had my brown hair and my nerdy uniform, I didn't even look like me any more anyway. And she said, 'Even when he's pissed he still looks capable of evil.' And that's when she said, 'You know what? In the end, it takes a thief to catch a thief.'

Six weeks after the fire James Arney came back to school. Everyone thought he would go to a new school, a million miles away from here, cos of Kathryn Cowell. But apparently his mum didn't wanna move. And he said he wanted to come back to be with his mates. He's got no memory of the fire at all, apparently. That's what everyone said. Couldn't even remember going to school that morning. Or getting up. I don't believe a fucking word of it. No one loses their memory like that, do they? Someone said that it's like a thing your brain does to stop you being upset, so you just blank everything out. Someone said he's glad he can't remember.

Since the police had cleared out of the languages block, the council had been rebuilding it but with new bits, like a lift and a ramp at the front with like some kind of fancy handrail. Then it went round the school that James Arney was coming back in a wheelchair until the skin on his legs had come back and that the school had been forced to put in special equipment for him so he could get around.

In the end, Kathryn Cowell and her gang were only suspended from school for one month. That's it. Even with the lighter the police didn't have enough evidence and Wino's dad made a lot of noise in the local paper about the rival gangs that met in the park right behind the school. So they came back off being suspended like nothing had happened. She had the fattest smile on her face. I'm not even lying. But underneath all the swaggering, the gang was like going round, trying to find out who planted the lighter. She'd told the police that she'd lost the lighter like ages ago. Said she'd dropped it in the park. That it wasn't her fault if some wanker had come and nicked her lighter then chucked it over the wall. They all said the same. Wino and Rob and all that lot said the same. It was really only a matter of time before they worked out that someone must have broken into the locker and planted the lighter. And only a matter of time before Wino put two and two together and came up with me.

I was totally fucking paranoid. If I heard someone running at school I would like tense my muscles ready for an attack. Or if there was shouting, I'd look for somewhere to hide. Passing Wino walking down the street nearly did my fucking heart in. It would thump really hard, like I had just run really fast in a marathon or something. And I got super super hot and then I couldn't see. It was like I was in a tunnel. And everything started whirling around and I couldn't lift my feet up any more. Like they were too heavy.

Ask me if I totally fucking regretted ever having anything to do with Kathryn Cowell's lighter.

I did then.

37

Sarah

Day Eight – 6 a.m.

'I have gossip.'

I can hear.

'What?'

I can hear but I can't feel anything. My hands have gone again.

'Pass me the chart, will you? Turns out the husband was an alcoholic. His liver was shot.'

'What, Sarah's husband? Really? Do you think she would have known that?'

Did I know that?

'Doubt it, not about the liver. Not unless she had X-ray eyes. He wouldn't have had any real symptoms yet – too young. His GP hadn't seen him for four years and then it was for a chest infection. But she must have known he was drinking really heavily.'

'Didn't any of the family mention it?'

'I guess we can ask the brother, since he's here all the time. That Ashley. What a creep! If I find him in here again on his own, I'm gonna tell Langlands. It's not right.'

Keep him away from me.

'We should tell Langlands. It's not normal.'

HE'S A FREAK. DON'T LET HIM NEAR ME. WHAT ARE YOU DOING?

'None of them seem to know much about Sarah, do they? Even her sister is pretty tight-lipped. Shame she doesn't adopt the same approach to Sarah's medical care and just let us get on with it.'

'I'll bet she knows more than she lets on.'

'I don't think Mum and Dad even know that things weren't all hearts and flowers – even though they didn't like him much. I think they all have just assumed that they'd only been married a couple of years. And newlyweds tend to still be nuts about each other.'

'For at least a week!'

They're both laughing.

'So he was an alcoholic and they were in marriage guidance – well …'

'Not the perfect couple, then.'

'Is there such a thing? You never really know what people are like, do you? People never really let on.'

I do remember Adam drunk. We were at a party. A lunch party. It was summer. This was before we were married. When we were still in the flat in Camden. He had gone an hour or so before me to the party, because I had been cleaning. The hall floor always needed cleaning. It was white. He said it collected dust. That it needed to be cleaned once a day, at least. I asked him to wait but he wouldn't. He wanted to get to the party. It was the weekend. It was Michael's party. Michael was his best friend. Michael was doing well. When I finally arrived, Adam was already quite drunk. Not falling-down drunk.

But as soon as I walked in I could tell. His eyes used to shoot off in different directions when he had had one too many. He was jabbing the air with his middle finger, a Marlboro Red in one hand, a can of Special Brew in the other. Chatting in a loud voice. Laughing with his head back and his mouth wide open. Eyes sparkling. Michael gave me that look that he always gave me when he was slightly embarrassed by Adam – slightly sorry and slightly guilty. When he saw me walk through the door, he shouted over the music. And he gave me a huge hug, like he hadn't seen me for ages. And he introduced me to everyone as his fiancée even though I didn't have a ring or anything. And everyone was cheering, saying they never thought Adam would settle down. And I must have special powers. It was only about half an hour later that I saw his mood had changed. I was talking to Michael's university friend. He did amazing portraits. He'd won a prize at the National Photographic Gallery. He asked me out once, ages ago. Adam knew. Adam was still talking animatedly to someone but his eyes were on me. All the time. Watching.

I managed to get Adam out of the party. Quite quickly in the end. He was beginning to get really shouty. I don't think he even realised that we were leaving. He was that off his head. He lurched against the walls of the staircase, like they had been built lopsided, and then he flung himself down the front steps and sprawled onto the pavement. He couldn't get up. He was laughing and coughing and dribbling out of the corner of his mouth. He crawled over to a lamp post and clawed his way to a standing position. Then he leaned there, for ages, with one hand on the lamp post and the other propped on his knee. His head was bowed over as he threw up. And I remember thinking, 'What am I doing here – with a drunk, bent over in the gutter? Why am I marrying him? Is this what my life is going to be like? Do I deserve this?' I don't remember how I got him into the car, but I do remember driving to a shop. One of those mini supermarkets, because he said he'd invited the entire party back to our house in three hours. Everyone. Like maybe twenty people. So I bought chickens. Three chickens. And some potatoes. And some lemonade, while he slept in the passenger seat. But when I left the supermarket, the car had gone. And I looked up the road and he was driving all over the place. Weaving like a lunatic in and out of the traffic. Thank God it was a Sunday. And I had these bags of chickens and potatoes. And our house was at least half an hour's walk. And I thought he was going to crash. I kept waiting for the bang. And I ran down the street. And I ran and I ran. And I kept thinking, around the next corner I'll see the crash. And he'll be dead. And his head will be bleeding all over the steering wheel. When I finally got back to the flat, the keys were in the lock and the door was still open. And he was asleep on the bed. Just passed out completely. Face down. And I shouted at him but he didn't hear me. I was hot. Crying. Crying from inside my stomach. When I'd stopped crying all I could hear was him snoring. And snoring. Like a pig. Like a fat, ugly pig. So I went to the kitchen and I took the chickens out of the bag and I put them in two roasting dishes. And I reparked the car, straight. I tidied up the flat again. When the smell of roast chicken started to creep into the sitting room, I realised that no one was going to come to a party that a falling-down drunk had invited them to. So I put away the potatoes. It was still Sunday and it was still sunny. So I thought I should do something. Something nice. I thought I would write a letter to my dad and tell him how lovely it was on a Sunday in Camden. And I could write to Sue, my friend in

Israel who picked mangoes on a kibbutz, and Ian in South Africa who teaches blind and deaf children. But I couldn't find the writing paper. I looked in the drawers and in the desk in the hall and it wasn't there. And I thought, well, it's getting late, he must be waking up now, so it won't matter if I wake him up, and I went to the bedroom and I clattered around in the wardrobe looking for the notepaper and it wasn't there either. So I looked in the chest of drawers and it wasn't there. And then, just as the late afternoon sun started making geometric patterns through the window onto the bedspread, I saw that Adam was blinking awake. And I said, 'Adam, do you know where the writing paper is?' And he just made a noise. So I said, 'Adam. Wake up! Can you just tell me where the writing paper is?' And he groaned. And then I thought, it must be in his office. In the box of papers he keeps under his desk. So I went to the back room and I crawled under his desk. He has this box. A leather box, which I had been given as a leaving present from my last job in the magazine publishing house. It was black leather. From Heal's. Nice. And I opened it and pulled out a load of photocopy paper and underneath was my notepaper. And underneath that were twelve porn magazines – twelve really ugly porn magazines. Not like soft stuff that you kind of turn a blind eye to but really awful, sad stuff. Stuff that you expect to find in a prison cell or in a murderer's house or something. Not in my flat. Not in my home. Not in my life. And I was sick. Sick. SICK OF IT ALL. And I was so cross and so sick and so I-don't-want-this-any-more. And I went back to the bedroom. Slowly. Deliberately, with all the nasty porn magazines. And I walked in and I threw them all at him. They landed half on him and half on the sunlight patterns on the bedspread. Various oversized breasts and bleached bumholes were bathed in a golden glow. And I said, 'What the fuck is this, Adam? WHAT THE FUCK IS THIS?' And he opened his eyes. And he moved his arm from under the magazines. And he looked at me steadily, not even at the magazines, just at me. And then, like out of nowhere, he leapt up off the bed. How could someone move that fast when they are drunk and half asleep? He grabbed me by my arm and swung me backwards against the chest of drawers and, as I fell, he grabbed my leg and like a sack of potatoes he threw me from one side of the room to the other. I just flew. And as I hit the wardrobe he fell back onto the bed. And as I slid down the mirrored door he fell back to sleep in the golden squares. And as I lay there on the carpet crying, wondering which of my bones were broken, he started to snore again. Like a pig. Like a fat, ugly pig.

The next day I got a taxi back from the hospital. They said I had to be collected by someone. That I couldn't go home alone. He didn't pick up the home phone. So I lied in the end and said Adam was just coming. He would be waiting outside in the car, I said. And the nurse let me off. I told her, Adam's not the kind of guy to leave his wife stuck at the hospital, is he?

He acted like nothing had happened. Even though my knee was bandaged and my arm was in a sling. He didn't say anything. And I didn't say anything either.

He just smiled and put his hand into his pocket. And lifted out a tiny box. He said, 'Let's get married.'

And my heart skipped a beat.

Stupid cow.

38

Kelly

Day Eight – 9 a.m.

It's Friday. An entire sodding week since I first went to wake Sarah up. And she's still not fucking awake. I've loaded my iPod. If we are allowed to go in today, I'm gonna take it. Mum is waiting to hear back from Tea and Tampons.

To be honest, I don't know what I'm most scared of. Without Sarah I've started to lose my fucking mind, let alone my balls. I've seen Wino going past a few times and that totally does my head in. Kathryn Cowell is larging it up at school apparently, off-the-scale thieving according to Laura Smith and Chloé Jeffries. Langlands is like a dog on fucking heat. Always marching up and down the street with his mobile stuck to his ear barking orders at fucking everyone. Every time he walks past our house he peers in our front window like he can see in. And Mum and I stand with our backs against the wall dunking our digestives into our tea. Meanwhile Adam's brother, previously AWOL, has shown up out of the fucking blue and is quite obviously 'up to something' while Langlands is gazing in the opposite direction. And I can't really ask about it because, if I do, they might wonder if I'm 'up to something'. This would definitely have been a moment to talk to Clare. She would know what to do. She would've.

I didn't tell you yet about Clare, did I? Not what happened in the end.

It was like a Thursday morning, just after French. It's when we usually go down to Burger King. We go out the art block door, that leads onto this street at the back of the school, which runs down into town, and if we go during first break they don't have a Year 13 on duty. We usually go at first break and get back in time for lunch. And then after lunch it's General Studies afternoon, which is LOL shite, so it's good to have something to look forward to before we have to sit in the main hall for like fucking hours listening to some poor, unfortunate twat go on about his loser life. We had this one guy in, a real god-botherer, who did this talk about drugs and how he had come off them and how evil drugs are and all that stuff, and he actually started crying halfway through his talk. I'm not even lying. In front of four hundred children he started crying. Awks. Even the teachers were like totally embarrassed. He cried and then he kind of pulled himself together and then at the end when we all clapped he started crying *again*. No kidding. They shouldn't invite people who are mentally ill to give talks at schools. How does that show a good role model? If anything, it makes you think he should go and take a few drugs and get out a bit. I think I'm more likely to take drugs after seeing him. Anyway, I texted Clare as usual during French to say meet by the art block and she didn't turn up. She'd gone a bit weird on me cos she said my hair was horrible now it was brown and what was wrong with White Platinum and I'd said, 'Nothing, I just felt like a change', and she'd said that I looked like Elly Nichols, who's like this total spaz in Year 9, and I said she should go fuck herself. She wasn't eating. That was her thing by then. Just Diet Coke. So she always said she didn't wanna come with us. But, like I said to her, we don't go down town for the food. We go for the fuck of it. Anyway, I thought she'd gotten over herself. So I texted her again and went and waited by the door. Then I sent a text to Hayley to see if she knew where she was and she said she hadn't even come in today. So I sent another text and she didn't reply so I went into prep for two lessons until lunch. The teacher overseeing prep was that English teacher Miss Broomfield who is such a fucking bitch. If she sees you using your phone she just takes it. She puts it in her bag and you can't have it back for a week. A fucking week! My mum says that it served me right when she took my last phone. It should be illegal to take someone's property for like a week. I bet it is as well. I mean what was I sposed to do without my phone? Cow. Anyway, cos it was Miss Broomfield I didn't try and text Clare until on the way into lunch, and she still didn't answer. Then I saw Camilla in the pasta queue and she said that Clare wasn't in at all, which I said was totally fine, but she can still pick up her phone, right, even if she is ill? So when I got home I said to my mum that Clare was off sick and she made me sit down, in the kitchen on Billy's stool, and she said that Clare wasn't sick. She said Clare had been attacked when she arrived at school early this morning. And that she was alright but she was gonna move away cos her mum was fed up of the school and everything and something should be done about them kids going around bullying people. And I was like, 'What happened? We all get bullied all the time. What's her problem?' And my mum said it was worse than that and I should just send a nice text to Clare and tell her I'd see her soon and stuff like that. Positive stuff rather than the 'Where the fuck are you?' that I'd sent like five minutes earlier. But I don't mind saying I was pissed off. She was leaving the fucking school and she wasn't even gonna tell me. Move away. Not a fucking word. I've been her best friend for like, what, over seven fucking years and she wasn't gonna talk to me about it. Ask me what I thought. I was never gonna get my clothes back either. Though obvs later I felt bad about that.

Apparently an ambulance had to be called to the school for her, and the police had come in just in case there was any trouble, but there wasn't. It must have been really early because the school managed to keep it quiet all fucking day. Things like that usually spread like fucking wildfire. There was no CCTV in the school. No proof of anything. And Clare wasn't saying a word, apparently. We were all texting each other in the evening. And everyone said it was Wino. And when I thought about it, he was acting like he'd done something cos when I saw him after lunch he'd been laughing and shouting and going, 'D'ya like my hair?' at Kathryn and everything. She just stood there with her arms folded, like smiling – how lunatic is that? No one knew what the fuck. It was like a big secret.

I waited for Sarah to arrive back from work so I could talk to her about it. There was this man over the other side of the street. I'd noticed him before. A few weeks back. He kept staring at their house. I don't know exactly how many times I'd seen him. Maybe four. I don't know. He always wore this brown leather jacket and he smoked the entire time. Like he'd finish a cigarette and right as it was like nearly at the filter he would light a new cigarette from it and start all over again. Sometimes, when he came at night, all you could see was this orange glow from the end of his fag. When Sarah pulled up in her car, he waited until she was locking the car door when he suddenly walked out from the shadows, crossed the road behind her and pulled her by her arm. She jumped fucking sky high and dropped her bag. He shouted in her face something about Adam and she shook her head. She knelt down to pick up her bag, never taking her eyes off his face. He looked like Middle Eastern. Or Greek. Maybe Indian. He had a moustache and slicked-back hair. He must have been like maybe forty or something. Quite small for a man. Little hands. Stone-washed jeans. A gold chain in his chest hair. Yuk. You know the kind of thing. He said something else, then let go of her arm and walked off, along the other side of the road where the streetlights are broken. Sarah locked her car. As she walked down her front path she looked up at my window. She moved her hand to wave then looked up at her own bedroom window and must have seen something there that stopped her. She went inside and I thought it best not to go round. I guessed Adam was there. It was that same night that Sarah fell down the stairs.

My mum was washing up, Billy had gone to bed and I was watching *Gogglebox* again, which my mum was shouting is 'the worst thing on TV, apart from *Undateables*', which we're actually not allowed to watch at all, even though it's like really funny and if the disabled people didn't want to be filmed going out on dates together they wouldn't be in it, would they? My mum says it's taking advantage of the differently abled. Who knows what the fuck that means? Anyway, the commercials came on, so when my mum came into the sitting room and asked me if I'd heard a crashing noise, I hadn't. The music was on too loud. So she turned down the sound, and we both stood in the hall and listened, cos my mum said the crashing came from next door, and suddenly the wall shook as their front door banged shut and then it was like totally silent. We watched in the dark through the net curtains in the front room as Adam got into the car and drove off. And my mum wiped her hands on a tea towel and told me to wait right there while she just checked to see if Sarah was OK and to not leave cos Billy was upstairs. So I stood in the hall with my forehead against the wallpaper tracing spirals with my finger, while I heard my mum ringing on Sarah's doorbell. She rang it three times and then I heard her call Sarah through the letterbox. I heard the squeak of the hinges as she pushed it open. Then she came racing back into our house to get Sarah's spare key, which was in the pot with the bees on, on the shelf in the kitchen. And, as she raced past me and nearly knocked me over, she shouted, 'Call an ambulance, Kelly. Do it now – 999. Tell them to be quick. Sarah's unconscious. She must have fallen down the stairs.'

Or he pushed her. We both knew that. But my mum will never involve the pigs.

Come to think of it, I seem to have spent an awful lot of fucking time in hospitals waiting for Sarah to wake up. That time, it was the hospital in Archway. The view from her room was of a massive roundabout. You could see a queue of traffic coming all the way down the hill for miles. She woke up that same evening, only really out for a couple of hours. She wasn't in a proper coma. Nothing like this time. She'd cracked her skull. She had black eyes and bruises behind her ears.

It's eight days now since Sarah was brought in here. The nurses promised she'd be OK after three. Maybe that's what they say to kids, just to make them feel better. I wish they'd just say the truth. No one ever says what they mean, do they? People just say what they think people want to hear. Don't they? The nurses don't say much any more. They just ask me stuff. I think they're nosey. What do they need to know about Adam for? He was a turd. End of. I'm not gonna tell them stuff about my best friend, am I? I'm not like that.

Sarah is my best friend now. At the time I was mad at Clare for never texting me back. I was mad that she changed her phone number without telling me. It seemed a bit random, don't you think? I mean it wasn't MY fault that Wino got to her. I didn't think it was anyway. No one at school knew what had really happened, and now that I know, I'm not gonna say, am I? I didn't find out what until Sarah told me later, like two weeks later when the whole situation got an awful lot worse.

She was all bandaged up still in the hospital, and my mum had been there too but she'd gone to phone Anna to make sure that Billy was OK and everything. And before she came back Sarah said, 'Did you hear about Clare?' and I said, 'I dunno, she's not answering her fucking phone.' And she goes, 'Kelly, Clare has died. She committed suicide.' And I'm like, 'Are you fucking mad?' And she's like, 'You have to stay calm. It's not your fault.' And I'm like, 'Why would you say that?' And she didn't say anything. She just looked at me. And I puked. On the floor. I thought she must be just talking crazy from the drugs and stuff. But Clare's mum had rung my mum who'd told Sarah who'd said not to tell me. That she would tell me herself. Turns out that once Clare had got over the shock of the attack she had waited until her mum was out of the way, run herself a hot bath, cut two deep lines with a razor blade down her forearms and waited while the water turned crimson. All because of Wino. All because of me. She'd told her mum everything. But said she would never tell the police. She was too scared to. But her mum knew.

On the day she got attacked Wino had stolen a Stanley knife from the art block. He got in early through the side door. Turns out he'd waited for her in the bike shed, like first thing in the morning. Clare was locking up her bike. He'd gone up behind her and without saying anything he grabbed hold of her ponytail and sliced it off. Sliced it off. Like still in one piece. Still in the hair band. So she had like no fucking hair. And he'd swung her ponytail round and round and he'd shouted at her about going in people's lockers and how it couldn't have been anyone but her and how she wasn't so clever now she hadn't got her fucking hair, was she? And then when she didn't say anything and she was just crying he said, 'Fuck off, Blondie', and told her that if he ever saw her again he'd fucking kill her. And Clare hadn't known what he was talking about. But she didn't say anything. Didn't say it wasn't her.

She'd told this to her mum. But only on the condition that her mum didn't tell the police cos if she did she'd say her mum made it all up. So her mum never even told the police.

And balls of Clare's White Platinum hair were all over the corridor outside the art block. Rolling up and down like tumbleweed. And we'd all seen them but none of us had even thought about what they were.

39

Sarah

Day Eight – 9 a.m.

'Brian, are you going to get me a cup of tea?'

'I thought they just asked you if you wanted one?'

'They did. But it was that woman again. The one I can't stand.'

'Why, what did she do?'

'She was rude, Brian. Rude to me. After everything that I'm going through.'

'What did she say?'

'Brian, does it matter what she said? What matters is, I want a cup of tea. And a biscuit, if they have them. A custard cream. Or a ginger nut. But not a rich tea. I hate rich tea.'

The door has clicked shut. The paper is rustling. My mother will be reading her horoscope. She swears by it. Won't set foot out of the door without checking Jonathan Cainer in the Daily Mail.

The door opens again. There is a slice of sound from the corridor beyond, before it closes again. The radio. Marvin Gaye. 'Sexual Healing'.

'There you go, June. A nice cup of tea. The pot was fresh.'

'Where are the biscuits?'

'They didn't have any.'

'Brian! I saw a big box of biscuits on the trolley.'

'You don't want to be eating the ones that have been travelling all around the hospital, for heaven's sake. They will be covered with germs. Covered! I should think you would pick up any number of diseases from eating those. They've all been breathed over by sick people.'

My dad is getting old. Ever since he gave up his job he has worried more and more about germs. And dust. He was quite normal when he was working. He had a job in York, at a law firm. Maybe he was a little OCD about his handkerchief being folded correctly or his meal being hot enough, or pasta being on the menu – he thought pasta was a middle-class affectation. But when he retired he began to overstress about little things. He would empty the kettle out completely before use, every time. He would run the tap for five minutes before he refilled it because he only wanted fresh water, not water that had been sitting in a pipe. He would end each day by wiping sterilising fluid over the kitchen surfaces. He boiled the dishcloths every Saturday morning and heat-steamed the kitchen floor on Mondays and Fridays.

'Brian. I think we should go home.'

'What do you mean we should go home? We can't go home. She hasn't woken up yet.'

Dad! Don't leave me here.

'I need to get back to the house. Our lives have just stopped here. One minute I was asleep, next minute we were hurtling down the motorway. It's like we have just stopped and we can't get anywhere. I need my routine back. I need to go home and get back to my routine. I need to sleep. Brian, do you hear me? I need to sleep. It's over a week since I slept in my own bed.'

Dad! Don't leave me here.

'June. Under no circumstances are we going home. You can sleep perfectly well at the Travelodge. The reason the victim support people pay for us to be at the Travelodge is so we can be here for our daughter. She's the victim, June, who needs support. It's all in the bloody name.'

Tell her, Dad.

'I've got a lot on next week, Brian. There's the Ladies' Breakfast at the tennis club on Wednesday. And Julie Grainger's wedding is next weekend. There's Dorothy House on Thursday. I need to get back for that too. We're down on the rota. I'm sorry, Brian, but we can't be here all the time. Carol can stay. She's good in these situations.'

'I don't understand what you're saying, June. Are you saying you think it's more important to go to your friend's daughter's wedding than it is to wait for your own daughter to come out of a bloody coma, because if that is what you are saying you can bloody well go home on your own.'

'Don't be ridiculous, Brian. I'm not going home on my own. You'll have to drive me. How am I going to get about if you don't drive me?'

'Let me get this straight. You think you're going to go back to life as normal, do you, despite the fact that your daughter is lying here on a life-support machine?'

'Not as normal, Brian, of course not as normal. But there's no need for us all to be here, is there? We can't do anything. We're just sitting about.'

Dad!

'And what about your friends? What do you think they will make of the fact that you are happy to leave your daughter on a life-support machine in London while you're busy baking fruit buns for a bloody coffee morning?'

'Well … we won't tell them, Brian. What's the point of telling them? They don't need to know our business, do they? They don't need to hear that Sarah has got mixed up with something like this. That our family is mixed up with some kind of *gang warfare.*'

'She was mugged, June. She is a victim of a mugging. She isn't mixed up in any kind of gang warfare.'

'And our Carol says she was after a divorce.'

'What? Sarah and Adam were getting divorced? June, what are you talking about now? You know full well what Carol is like. Take no notice. She always dramatises everything. She always winds you up about Sarah. For heaven's sake, June, your daughter is in a coma.'

'And if she wakes up, we'll come back!'

'What do you mean, if? What do you mean, IF, June?'

That's it. That's all they said. They've gone. As it has sunk in I realise that I'm not surprised. My mother is not the kindest of women, well, not when it comes to me. She's more interested in her tennis friends and her horoscope and her old ladies, things that she can get credit for. There's not much reflected glory from someone like me, quiet, dull, non-achiever, bit of a loser. She wouldn't understand that her attitude was what turned me that way. Why did I think that? Why do I blame her? I don't know.

My dad told me then that he loved me. She'd already gone. He said I was the most beautiful girl in the world. He whispered it in my ear. And he left me.

And I don't know if he's coming back.

40

Kelly

Day Eight – 4.30 p.m.

The police are here again. My dad, when he was here, he used to actually call them pigs to their faces. Even before they arrested him. I don't think pigs like the Irish. Who do they like? Themselves. But my mum tells me off if I call them pigs. Actually, my dad used to call them fucking pigs. My mum would wop me one if I said that. She's crashing around the kitchen with Great Auntie Betty's best cups and Detective Inspector Twathead is doing his Sherlock impersonation in the front room. He has a laptop. Fuck my life, he looks like a twat.

Mrs Tea and Tampons is here too. She's also in the front room. She's on the edge of the sofa looking like she's about to melt. She has art-teacher earrings on – you know, too big, too loud – and fat crusty sandals that look like they were made with fucking potato peelings or something. I'm not even lying. Sarah would have been pissing herself laughing at them. They didn't come together, Mrs T&T and Twathead. She had an appointment. Twathead just turned up. She's sposed to be here to talk through any 'issues' we might have concerning Sarah, and to explain what will happen after her next medical assessment. I dunno if she would have told us all that if Sarah's mum and dad hadn't just fucked off home yesterday. But since we are on the visiting rota – they have a rota so that there's always someone there talking to her, and her sister's fucking crazy, and Sarah's in a coma, so I think they're running low on victims to support. But Langlands has crashed the party and urgently needs to 'interview the friends and acquaintances of Adam'. He also wants to know about Ash. Adam's brother.

'But I don't know any friends or acquaintances of Adam. Or Ash. I didn't even know he had a brother,' says my mum. 'Would you like milk?' she smiles, hovering with the milk in a jug with like totally vile pink roses all over it. I'm leaning against the wall opposite the open door of the front room, my arms behind my back, in my school uniform again.

'Kelly, get the biscuits would you, please,' she says in that posh voice she saves for Father O'Shea.

'Er, no, thank you, Mrs McCarthy,' says Langlands. 'Can we just get on with this?'

'Is that no to the milk or no to the biscuits or no to both?' she smiles brightly.

'Mrs McCarthy!' says Langlands, getting hot and red. He's got drips of sweat along the top of his forehead where his hair used to be.

'Brenda,' says Mrs Tea and Tampons, 'the Detective Inspector has got to do this entire road by lunchtime. Can you think of anyone who was friends with Adam, or who knew Adam well, so we can find out if there was anyone who might have had some kind of grudge against him?'

'Mrs McCarthy,' says Langlands, looking like he's swallowing a wasp, 'I'll be honest with you.' (Sarah always said never to trust anyone who said, 'I'll be honest with you.' She said it always meant they were about to tell you a big fat lie.) 'We're following up on some excellent leads on this investigation so far. But we need to know more about Adam. We need to speak to the people he was in contact with on the day that he died. And obviously without any kind of statement from Sarah, it's become necessary to go back over some old ground to try to piece together his last movements. And hers.'

'She's not dead, don't forget, Detective Inspector', and she closed the door and left me standing in the hall, listening through the wall with the spirally wallpaper.

I don't know why my mum is lying about the divorce papers. I mean not lying exactly, but sort of not exactly telling the truth either. Langlands keeps saying things like, 'Did Sarah tell you that she was unhappy in her marriage? Did Sarah tell you that she wanted a divorce? Did you know she was going to mediation with Adam, at all? Did she ever tell you that her husband was violent?' And my mum just goes, 'Not to my knowledge. Not to my knowledge. Not to my knowledge.' I guess if she had to swear on the Holy Bible, if they actually got a Bible out and made her put her hand on it or whatever it is you're sposed to do, she might decide that 'the great vengeance and furious anger of the Lord' was more of a match than old Twathead.

I mean, anyone can see he's asking the wrong fucking question. If there's one thing that he could have got to know about Sarah by now, if he'd sat down and thought about it for a second, it's that the last thing she is ever gonna do is tell anyone anything she thinks. She's the most private person I ever met. We only knew about Adam because we heard it with our own ears. And saw the cuts and bruises. I can never even for one second imagine Sarah saying, 'Oh hi, Brenda. My husband hit me', or 'Hi Brenda, guess what? My husband just broke my leg and now I think I must really get a divorce.' She's not like that. She never tells anyone anything about what she feels. If I ever asked her anything like that, she always said that Adam was a good man. She always said she wasn't quite sure what she felt. She always said, 'How does anyone actually decide how they feel about anything?' It wasn't easy for her to persuade herself that Adam might kill her one day, if she didn't get away from him. The hours in mediation, on her own, gave her a new perspective, she said. She started to see that a life without him was possible. And that a life with him would end prematurely – as in, her own life. She said 'prematurely', not me. But I know what it means. And I understand what it meant to Sarah.

My mum doesn't actually know any of that. So not just the wrong questions – it's really rather fucking funny that Langlands is asking totally the wrong person.

He's getting really arsey now. He's not getting anywhere and he knows it. There's a snap as he closes his laptop and the clink of his cup hitting the saucer. He's picked up his car keys.

'I'm only sorry I can't be of more help,' Mum says as she opens the front-room door. 'Is your car nearby, Detective Inspector?

Cars have a nasty habit of going missing around here, but you'll know that won't you, you being a policeman? You must get complaints all the time.'

'I don't deal in car crime, Mrs McCarthy. I deal in killings.'

'Did you not hear about when Sarah and Adam's car got nicked? From right out the front of their house. Look, is that your BMW? Theirs was parked almost exactly where yours is now.'

'That would go through to the car crime division, Mrs McCarthy. As I say, not my area. Why – do you know who nicked it, Mrs McCarthy?'

'Well, how would I know?' she says. 'I'm not a detective inspector, am I?'

'So you have no idea?'

'It was one of them gangs, Detective Inspector. You know what it's like around here. Adam chased them all the way down the road, though. Didn't catch them, but he chased them all the way down to White Hart Lane. He got the car back the same day. Not quite sure what he threatened them with, but whatever it was it worked.'

'Don't you think that information is relevant to our investigation, Mrs McCarthy? Don't you think you could have mentioned that before?'

He looks like he's about to explode.

'You don't deal in car crime though, Detective Inspector, do you? Plus,' she adds with a smile as she walks down the front path and opens the gate, 'you didn't ask.'

'I believe the crime wasn't solved, you see. So no one will know who did it. This area is full of gangs. The police mainly don't get involved. Don't even bother to come out …' she says, turning back up the front path. And as she closes the front door behind her, she adds under her breath, 'And when they do show up they just act like fucking pigs.' I'm sure that's what she said. She can't see me standing at the top of the stairs.

41

Sarah

Day Eight – 6 p.m.

I don't believe in God so I don't know why a chaplain is here. He's praying right next to me. Apparently the lord is my shepherd, therefore I will not want. Could've fooled me. It sounds so creepy this close. Don't you have to sign something before they allow people in like this? Carol wouldn't have signed anything. She doesn't believe in God either. When it comes to God, I think she might actually go the other way.

'Evening, Sarah. The mighty Reverend Cheston has gone. Time for a sponge bath.'

I love Beth. She's the nicest of the nurses. She must be older than the others. She's the only one who doesn't treat me like I'm dead already.

'So your sister is coming back in a little while, and then your good friend Mr Malin is on his way. So let's see if we can open our eyes, shall we. C'mon, Sarah. You need to get busy now.'

She's always so nice. Not patronising.

'Evening, Carol. Do you want to come back in a while? We have to do a bath before Mr Malin gets here.'

'I've just come to get something out of Sarah's locker. Her bag is in there, right?'

What's in my bag?

'Yes, they brought the bag in with her. Unusual that. One of those policewomen checked it and they definitely took the credit cards, ID and cash. But once it turned into a murder case, you'd have thought they wanted the bag back for evidence.'

'They haven't even tried to use the cards. Weird that. You'd have thought they would've used them straight away. Cleaned out the accounts before anyone knew about it.'

'Maybe they sold them abroad – that's what quite often happens. We had one lady in here whose cards got used to buy thirty-five thousand dollars' worth of garden furniture in New York. The bank didn't notice. She was eighty-eight.'

'You wouldn't think it was possible to spend that much on gardens, would you? I'm trying to find these divorce papers that everyone seems to be going on about. Did the victim support woman ask you about them?'

'She said that the police were trying to get a copy off Sarah's solicitor. What's the big deal?'

'I dunno. The solicitor says it's a breach of her client trust or something. I've looked at their house. I suddenly thought maybe they've been in her bag all the time.'

'That would be hilarious. The amount of times Langlands has stood in here.'

I can hear them rattling around near the bed.

'Here they are! So, sister darling, what's all this then?'

'What is it?'

'Well! So she was going for a divorce. Unreasonable behaviour. Good for you, little sister. Finally found your balls, did you? Hardly surprising, given he was a psycho.'

'Was he?'

'Oh, I don't know. She never said much. She hasn't ever said much. She's just one of those private types. Bit of a victim really. She wasn't like that as a child, though. She was much more fun when she was little. There are films of her playing in the garden when she looks so happy, so confident. And then when she was about seven she started to become ... oh, I don't know, withdrawn? Moody? She had this accident, apparently. No one talks about it. I was away at school at the time and if you ask my mother, she refuses to accept that anything ever happened. She said once that Sarah made it all up. It all came to a head when Sarah cut herself quite badly. She was cutting all her hair off at the time. With garden shears. We moved after that. Went to live in a house in the city. But ever since, Sarah has been different. You know, a bit sullen, serious, unbelievably private ... Listen, I'm gonna split. I'll be back after her bath. I want to catch up with Malin.'

She leaves. And everything starts to get silent again. An accident! There was never an accident. I'm sinking into blackness. The neighbour. Suddenly I remember, and everything gets even worse.

Mr Eades. The man in the garden. The Community Care man everybody loved. He'd had some kind of mental breakdown or something. And the neighbours had all adopted him as their little

*project. Help out Mr Eades. Give Mr Eades a purpose. And my
mother calls it an accident.*

*He was there, in the shed, every day. I don't think you can call a
disgusting old man showing his ugly dick to a small girl an accident,
can you? I don't think closing the shed door behind the little girl and
forcing his disgusting penis inside her little white pants can happen
by accident, can it?*

I'm swimming in blackness.

*His old crooked hands, his long muddy nails, his cracked skin.
Do you understand? He said I'd* ASKED *for it. He said, 'Pretty little girls are the worst.' He said, 'Pretty little girls only want one
thing.' He said, 'Pretty little girls use their pretty blond hair and
their long eyelashes', and that running to his shed every afternoon
to play with the pots 'is what wicked girls do when they want something else', and it meant it was all my fault and my mother would
say so too, 'so don't you dare say anything' and 'don't you dare
forget to come back tomorrow or your mummy will tell your daddy
what a nasty little girl you are'.*

*I did not have an accident. I had four years of physical and
mental abuse.*

*I don't want to remember any more. It's very dark. It's very
silent. I'm disappearing completely.*

42

Kelly

Day Eight – 9 p.m.

'I'm sorry to hear about your friend.'

'What friend?'

Beth is nice but, fuck, she seems to find out everything.

'The girl who committed suicide. Was it just a month ago?'

'It was a while ago, actually. Yeah. Bad times.'

She's found me in the Family Room with a carton of Ribena and cheese and onion Walkers cos the vending machine in the hall has run out of smoky bacon. I've come to wake Sarah up because, seriously, it's too fucking long. I'm not even lying. She's been out for what, nine days? What am I sposed to do? Beth says I have to get on with my life. Stop coming here.

I say that I don't know how to make any decisions without Sarah. And Beth says it's my life and I have to grab it with both hands and be brave.

Be brave.

Beth's sat down for a minute cos she says they're waiting for a new patient who hasn't turned up yet but as soon as the ward doors open she'll have to go cos it's a car accident and car accidents are usually the worst thing they get up here and they always have to hurry cos it could be life or death. So I start trying to explain what Sarah is like but it's difficult for two reasons. One, Sarah has changed so much lately. Not since the accident, I don't mean that, cos obvs she's changed since the accident. No, I mean that she changed a lot in the two years or so since I met her. Before that it was like she had a light coming out of her. Like, seriously, people just really loved her, for no reason. Or hated her. There were people who found her too bright, too positive maybe. Jealous people. I'm not even joking. I saw a woman go up to her once and spit in her face. Seriously. Like for no reason. She was sitting on a bench in Manor House tube station and she goes up to her and says, 'Pride comes before a fall', then spat a fat gob on her cheek. Sarah says she was smiling about something funny at the time and maybe the woman thought she was laughing at her. She shouted it all the way down the platform. And another woman just said 'bitch' to her when she walked past her, like under her breath, and she didn't even know her. That wasn't even in Tottenham. That was in Bond Street. Mainly, though, it was people who just kind of fell for her. There was another time at some concert or other, when this guy walked right up to her and said that she was the most beautiful woman he had ever seen. Like out of the blue. Weird, right? It wasn't because she was beautiful beautiful. You wouldn't have looked at her and said Kate Moss or Cara Delevingne or anything. She was sort of beautiful from the inside. She had this kind of sparkle. She wasn't really aware of it herself. She didn't act like she was beautiful.

There was the time in this coffee shop. I was telling Beth. Seriously this actually happened. A new Caffè Nero opened in

Wood Green and Sarah said we should go for a hot chocolate. This was like a year ago, before they closed off the High Street to make it pedestrianised. She didn't actually have a hot chocolate. She only drinks skinny latte. She said she had to meet Adam later but that we could go for like half an hour this one Saturday morning. When we got there you had to queue up cos it was new and there were like a fucking million people there and I think they'd done this thing where they'd given out vouchers or something so you could get a free drink. Anyway, we were standing in this queue when this kid starts staring at us. He was a total Downie. He had these great big silver trainers that looked like they were right out of Transformers or something, and a fat brown spot with a hair growing out of it right in the middle of his cheek. So I go 'retard alert' and Sarah goes, 'You can't say something like that when the person is *actually* a retard.' And he gets to our place in the queue and he kind of blurts, 'Excuse me?' and she goes, 'Yeah?' And he goes, 'Excuse me, do I know you? I think I know you.' And she's really polite back and goes, 'No, I don't think you know me', and she looks away. And she presses her elbow against my arm really hard so I start to laugh. The bloke turns to walk off and we both kind of sigh with relief when he comes right back and he says, 'What's your name?' And she goes, 'I'm Sarah. This is my friend Kelly and you don't know us but it's been really nice to meet you.' I wouldn't have said that. I would've said 'Go fuck yourself, you weird fuck', but Sarah says if you are horrible to people it says more about you than it does about them. And he goes, 'Well', and he kind of looks up at the ceiling. And he goes, 'Well, I love you.' That totally did it for me. I was like wetting myself.

I mean what kind of fucked-up person goes up to a complete fucking stranger and says I love you. Sarah started to laugh too. And she blushed, not because of the 'I love you' thing, more cos she didn't wanna laugh in the guy's face cos that's rude and she wouldn't want to be rude, not even to a retard. And she said, 'I think you'd better go and sit back down.' And he did.

So we got our drinks. My hot chocolate had whipped cream on top with chocolate sprinkles. It was a lot more chocolaty than the one you get in Starbucks. Sarah said the Caffè Nero logo looked like it said 'Caffè Nerd'. We were laughing about that and then we got sidetracked by my English Lit homework. We were doing *The Great Gatsby* and I was saying how Gatsby was this great big romantic hero and Sarah was saying that he wasn't much better than a stalker, when, guess what, the kid comes back. He must have been about eighteen, I dunno. He acted like he was about seven. We didn't get his name. We never got that far. If I had to guess a name for him I would say Malcolm but that's only cos there was this boy at my nursery called Malcolm who was like four years older than everyone else and he had a nurse with him all the time and he had something wrong with him that made him want to hold his toy car really close to his eye and make its wheels spin around. Anyway, Malcolm was back and he went right up behind Sarah and shouted right in her ear, 'I want to marry you.' And she nearly fell off her fucking chair it made her jump so high. And cos I'd seen him coming I could do nothing but laugh out loud and then Sarah started to laugh and then stopped. Cos at that moment Adam appeared. Now you could almost forgive Adam for being cross cos, for him, all that's happened is he has walked into this cafe, and seen some weird-looking guy go up behind his wife and say something that has like so shocked her that she's nearly fallen off her chair. As he walked up to the table the weirdo realised that there was some bloke heading his way so he started to try to get away but there were too many people. The whole place goes quiet. And Adam goes to Sarah, 'What were you doing with him?' but he's shouting, really angry. And she just shook her head, like as if to say don't worry about it. But that just made him more angry. And he said, 'What the fuck did you do, Sarah?' By now the whole cafe is silent. And I said, 'He's just a weirdo, Adam. He said he's in love with Sarah, that's all. But he's just a Downie.' And Sarah looked at me like steadily, like not cross with me but just like, 'Shut the fuck up.' Across the cafe a tired-looking woman was starting to panic. She was searching for someone, was starting to panic. She'd been staring into her coffee, stirring it round and round, and the silence had jolted her out of it. When she saw Malcolm her eyes widened like she was scared. She could see there was something going on. People had started to stand up. An old man stretched out his hand to Adam and shouted, 'Stop it, young man. Just stop it!' but Adam wasn't even listening. Adam had got the boy by his collar and was pulling so tightly on it that Malcolm, or whatever his name was, was turning blue. Spit was dripping from the side of his mouth. Adam was holding a clenched fist at the side of Malcolm's head like he was gonna hit him. Sarah was screaming at Adam to stop but Adam wasn't even looking at the weird kid, he was staring straight at Sarah as if to say, now look what you made me do.

Something snapped in Sarah that day. We were still close, me and her. But she switched off. She got her hair cut. She stopped wearing make-up. She got thin. She was like a shadow of herself.

And then the buzzer goes on the door, and Beth is standing up looking fucking shocked actually and backs to the door and says, 'And then what happened?' And I say that the boy was OK, and that the tired-looking woman was never gonna press charges, and that then Adam took Sarah home. So nothing happened really. No one said anything. I don't think anyone ever actually even called the police. It was Wino's brother, the weird kid, and the tired-looking woman was Wino's mum. Maybe that's why no one called the police. Or maybe it was because, in Tottenham, everyone thinks that the gangs will sort it out better than the police ever will.

I didn't say the last bit to Beth. She's gone. The trolley has arrived. The woman on it is groaning. She's the car crash. You almost feel guilty about being healthy when you see something like that. Hospitals do strange things to your head. I wish I'd got to Sarah's rooms before the car crash arrived because Detective Inspector Langlands has appeared with his usual bodyguards and is following the trolley up the corridor. I shrink back into my chair with my Ribena. When everything seems quiet I lean over the back of my chair and poke my head out of the door and look up the corridor to the nurses' station where I can see Langlands talking to Beth. She is nodding towards the room I'm in, looking concerned, and Langlands starts heading my way. It's too late to leave so I crawl back into the chair in the far corner – the drug smuggler's chair.

'Kelly, is it?'

'Yeah,' I say.

'Kelly, have you been entirely straight with us?'

'What?'

'Well, you've been here nearly every day just about since Sarah arrived. Perhaps you know more about Sarah than you've let on? Shouldn't you be at school?'

'I should be at home by now, actually. You're fucking right. See ya.'

I put my blazer on and try to walk past him.

'That's not like you, Kelly, is it? Swearing? Teenage attitude?'

'Goodbye, Detective Inspector. I have to go.'

He's standing in my way.

'Did you know, for instance, Kelly, that your friend Sarah has been going to baseball practice for the past year?'

'Baseball? Sarah? Really? Good for her. If you see my mum tell her I've gone home, would ya?'

I had swung my satchel over my shoulder and I was running. Through the double doors. Down the corridor towards the cafeteria where my mum is belting up the corridor towards me. She can't walk in those shoes. She should give up and wear boring shoes like other mums. When I tell her Langlands is in the ward she stops in her tracks. She turns around fast and comes outside with me and we both find her car, which she's lost again, in the multi-storey and drive home. She says she'll call Mrs Backhouse to get me off school for next week too. I'm fucked if I wanna see Kathryn Cowell right now, considering what I need to do. Be brave. I can't wait for her to wake up any longer. I need to finish what Sarah and I started.

43

Sarah

Day Nine – 6 a.m.

You don't realise until you have no memories at all that you are a product of them. When you are an empty sheet of paper, you can't even relate to yourself let alone to anyone else. You have no north and south. No right or left. You don't know how to think and you don't know what you think. Now that I have remembered things – I think – I wonder if I was better off not knowing.

And then I can't help but wonder what kind of a life I would have had if the five-year-old me had acted differently. Had looked different. Had not befriended a kindly old gardener who let her play in his shed with the old pots.

What would I have been like if it hadn't happened? Would I have been happier, sunnier, more successful – more like my sister?

I can remember now, quite clearly, standing behind the kitchen door in the shadows, looking out into the garden towards the dark trees at the bottom and the hedge with the shed. I can remember thinking, this proves that everything is evil! There aren't fairies or gnomes or magic toadstools. There can't even be a Father Christmas. There's no unicorns or fairy dust or magic shoes or flying beds. Not if nasty people can do nasty things and you can't stop them. And I told my dad. And even though my mother told him I was a liar, and I was just making something dreadful up to be dramatic, the next thing I knew was that I wasn't allowed in the garden any more, not unless my dad was there, and suddenly we were moving house, and suddenly we had no garden and no need for gardeners ever again. And my mum wouldn't look at me. She said what would people think? Why had I wanted to shame her family?

I'm not telling you this for sympathy. I don't ever tell anyone anything. I'm not one of those people who lets life happen to them. I just think it's important to know what happens to pretty little girls. Better not to be a pretty little girl.

I bet, up to now, you thought that pretty people have an easier ride in life. Everyone thinks that. The not-pretty people think that. Pretty people don't. If you're pretty it goes one of two ways: you're either coveted or despised – coveted by men, despised by women. Not all of them, obviously, but a lot of them. I've been avoided by women because, and they've actually said this, I make them look worse. I've been spat at by women in the tube station, for looking too happy. I was slapped once for eyeing up someone's boyfriend – I didn't know who she was talking about. I've been passed over for promotion for being lightweight – i.e. pretty. Then you get the underhand spite. These women claim to like you. Some of them genuinely think they do. I used to work with this woman, Leila, who was frankly as fat as a house and not attractive by anyone's imagining. The postroom boys used to say that she'd fallen out of the ugly tree and hit every ugly branch on the way down. But she was nice. She seemed nice. She obviously knew she was no oil painting. She was forever hiding under her fringe, fluffing it out a bit with her fingers to try to make it look thicker and more come-to-bed-ish. As if. Anyhow, everyone thought it was terrific that she was so especially friendly to all the especially pretty girls. But after a few times of being introduced as the gorgeous Sarah, the lovely Sarah, the beautiful Sarah, I realised that that was her way of undermining me. Anyone she felt remotely intimidated by, because they were prettier than her, she'd introduce as lovely or beautiful. As though that was all they were. Just a pretty face.

Men are a different story. Men have not really progressed from cavemen. They just want to own you like a rock or a stick or a motorbike or a watch or something. They want to win you, they want to enjoy you and then they want to own you, and when they can't own you they want to hurt you. In that order. Every time. Now I remember everything. I remember friends' boyfriends or even husbands whispering how much they wanted to fuck me, with their partners standing in the same room. Remember them pushing themselves against me while their wives were right next to them. Remember being felt up by weirdos on buses, falling asleep once on a train and waking up to find a man wanking over me. I remember being stalked by people I didn't know and people I did. On the beach, in shops, in cafes, in cinemas, at concerts, on planes, I remember complete strangers telling me they wanted to marry me. I am a walking, talking honeypot. I was.

And when I fall for the patter, when I'm coerced and manipulated into thinking that this is going to be the right man, the same thing always happens. Nice, less nice, controlling, unkind, violent. And then you can't get away. And you can't change the way that people are. And men can't help themselves. It's like they are hardwired. You have to change yourself. Keep yourself plain, keep your friends few, keep your answers short and your eyes down.

What about Adam? Yes, what about Adam? I know what you're thinking. Not so astute then, was I? Look, I thought I'd found someone different. Someone who wasn't trying to consume me but would just love me, not for what I looked like, but for what I was inside. For a while it worked. We got the house in South Tottenham. We painted it in nice colours, we agreed on wool carpets and hung nice velvet curtains. We had good jobs and a nice car. But I was wrong. Perhaps the drinking changed him. When we first started going out he didn't drink, not so much. But when he lost his job he started drinking at ten in the morning. Maybe the weed twisted his mind. After our first year of marriage he was smoking all day and all night. He would come to bed at five. He would be drunk and stoned. I would ball up the duvet tightly under my chin, and sleep on and off, waiting for his footsteps on the stairs. If I was lucky he'd pass out on the sofa, sometimes next to a pool of sick on the carpet. If I was unlucky he would come into the bedroom. And when I heard the door swing open, my hands, my top lip and the back of my neck would start to sweat. And he would snap on the overhead light, lurch towards the bed and then pull as hard and as fast as he could on the duvet, so that it whipped out from under my chin and burned the skin on my neck and tore at my nails. In that state his eyes couldn't focus. His hair would be as wild and twisted as his eyeballs. His voice would be low and threatening and slurred. Sometimes, as he tried to grab me across the bed, he would fall on his elbow, and just the feeling of the mattress and the sheets and the need for sleep would overwhelm him. Sometimes he would sit in the chair by the window, just for a second, just to catch his breath, and while he decided what was to come next, his head would tip forward and within a second or two he would be snoring and dribbling onto his shirt. And sometimes, if I tried to make a dash for the door, he'd catch me by my ponytail as I slid across the mattress, and wind my hair around his hand and drag me back onto the bed. When you cry, lying on your back, the tears go in your ears.

I had my hair cut.

I don't go around telling anyone all that because I don't want people to decide what I am, based on that. I'm not defined by being a victim. I'm not defined by being pretty. I'm defined by being me.

When I went to see the solicitor about getting a divorce I wasn't going to tell her anything about all that either. It felt disloyal. The solicitor was young. I was her first case. But she said I didn't even have any grounds for a divorce unless I told her something. I thought I would get away with a not-so-specific version but she said that the legal system doesn't work that way. The law states that you have to have proper reasons to end a marriage.

I was away the morning the postman delivered the brown envelope containing my divorce papers to Adam. I was away for a few days. At a conference in Liverpool. He wasn't going to let me go but I said I would lose my job if I didn't. He needed my money. I'd had to give him the address of the conference, the address of the hotel and the names of the people I was travelling with. He'd given his permission. My mobile started vibrating at 8:49, which is about two minutes after the postman usually arrives. Adam would have had to sign for it. My phone kept vibrating until about four in the afternoon when it suddenly went quiet. That was the point that I got really nervous. I don't know why I thought he would behave any differently from how he usually behaved. I suppose I thought that something legal might make him see that I was stronger than he thought I was. That I could stick up for myself, after all.

I'd already told him that we should break up. One morning when his hangover had worn off, I'd told him that I needed to be on my own for a while. I'd practised saying that in front of the mirror. I'd said that I thought it would be best for both of us. To start off with he thought I was kidding. He laughed. And I considered laughing the whole thing off but I had got that far. I had practised so long. So I said, 'No, I'm not joking.' Then he broke down and wept. He begged me. He wiped his eyes and his nose on the cuff of his denim shirt. He said he couldn't live without me. Then he stopped crying and said surely I couldn't live without him. He said I wouldn't last a second, that I was stupid. He said I was a joke. He said, seriously, if I thought I could live without him, then go on then, get a solicitor. I don't think he thought I would.

I was going back to my hotel room at the Travelodge to call Brenda. I thought she might have seen him. I'd seen one of those pre-mixed gin-and-tonics in the minibar earlier. I swiped the card through the door handle. The room felt hot. The windows were the sort that don't open but the air con had been on. The bed was made. The bathroom light was on. I hadn't left it on.

He was sitting in the chair in the corner by the net curtains. He was smiling. He'd told the reception desk that he was there to give me a surprise. He'd shown them his passport just in case. Married. He said it was a special anniversary. He'd asked them to bring champagne. There was a plastic champagne bucket. The ice had long gone and the bottle was sitting sadly in the tepid water. He untwisted the metal cage, still smiling, and flipped out the cork. There were matching plastic wine glasses with hollow stems on a pink plastic tray. He said, 'You know, we are actually celebrating.' He said, 'This is the start of a new chapter in our marriage.' He said, 'I'm prepared to be fair', and that if I came home now, like right this very second, he would not kill me, yet, or my dad and my mother, or my friends. He handed me back the divorce papers, in the same manila envelope that my solicitor had sent them in. I folded them and put them in my bag. I took a sip of the warm champagne from the cheap glass and waited for the inevitable. I don't remember what happened next. Not now. Not yet.

I have given up. I don't expect to wake up. Not really. I'm not even sure I want to any more. Even if I did wake up, I wouldn't make a good invalid. And my mother would make a rotten Florence Nightingale. Imagine if you were stuck in a bed all day with a bagful of urine by your side and a tube shoved down your throat.

I don't want that kind of life. It's not any kind of life. They won't keep me alive much longer. I can't see, I can't feel, I can't hear.

I am sinking again into nothing.

Down into blackness.

It seems safer.

And then Kelly's face appears.

Kelly.

Right in front of my face.

Kelly.

Right there.

So bright.

44

Kelly

Day Nine – 7 p.m.

I'm in the cafeteria. Let me tell you what just happened. You won't fucking believe it.

I was in talking to Sarah, like normal, all about fucking everything, and Beth came in. If I'm honest, I'm a bit pissed with Beth cos she obvs told Langlands about the whole Adam and Caffè Nero thing, which got him totally wound up.

My mum was like fucking furious about it. Said the pigs are fucking stupid if they can't even find a fucking proper suspect and that the trouble with them is that they have to appear to solve the case and they don't really care who goes down for it so long as someone does and we have to be careful not to lead the police up the fucking garden path, cos she says, if it's possible for the police to go up a fucking garden path, they'll go up a fucking garden path. Anyhow, Beth comes in and says that Langlands has been going on about CCTV cameras. She was being all nice and everything, asking me about school and stuff. But then she said that, on the night of the mugging, the camera in White

Hart Lane near the park was out, which he thinks is like totally suspicious but, like, what's he even talking about? Is he fucking Denzel Washington or something? Does he seriously think there's some organised crime to dismantle CCTV, like ninjas in masks climbing up lamp posts or something? I told Beth. 'It's a game,' I said. 'Everyone does it.' I told her about the gum on the lens and the baseball bat. 'And every time the council has to come back to put up new ones.' The council knows the gangs do it, but the police don't do anything about it. They don't do anything about gangs in South Tottenham, full stop. My mum says the gangs get more respect than the pigs anyway. So Beth says Langlands thinks no CCTV footage is like a fucking lead or something. Like it means something. Genius. The CCTV that does work, at the junctions each end of the road, apparently shows no one suspicious-looking on the streets at the time, so Langlands thinks the gang, if there was a gang, he said, must have peeled off into the park. 'And we all know who owns the park.' I said that to Beth. She said, 'Kathryn Cowell', and I nodded. I've taught her well.

And she said I should tell Detective Inspector Langlands. And I said I might. But I didn't need to, cos I know for a fucking fact that she will.

Anyway that wasn't the good bit.

My mum finally arrived. She'd got a CD player out of the attic and wanted to try out her Take That CD. Jesus. And she starts having a go at Beth, who was doing Sarah's physio, cos she said that Langlands is going up the garden path. And she said that he should go out and find the real killer and the person who did this to Sarah instead of wasting everyone's time. And Beth said we shouldn't talk about it in front of Sarah. And my mum said that, next thing we knew, Langlands would be saying that Sarah killed Adam, and maybe Beth should check while she's doing the physio to see if Sarah had extendable rubber legs cos that would be what she would need if she was gonna whack a really tall bloke.

Beth laughed and gave Sarah's ankles a pull and we all laughed and then Beth went to get some clean towels and my mum went to get a screwdriver cos the fuse had blown in the plug of the CD player and I was standing next to Sarah and then guess what happened. This is the good bit. You won't believe me. Her eyes moved. Seriously. Her fucking eyes moved.

I was like, 'Sarah. Your fucking eyes just moved.'

And I got my hand and I moved it in front of her face like close to her eyes.

And I was like, 'Do it again, Sarah. Do it again!' Like shrieking.

And I moved my hand from left to right, right to left and her eyes followed my hand. And I was like, 'Sarah's waking up.'

And I was like, 'Beth! Fuck, Beth! Come back, Mum! Sarah, you're waking up. Do it again.'

And Beth ran in to find out what I was screaming about and she was smiling, but saying not to get too excited. And my mum ran in and just started crying and laughing at the same time. It was amazing.

It was me who woke her up.

I woke her up.

But Beth said that I ought to leave her alone with Sarah for a bit so that she could organise some checks and that I really ought to go and get a cup of tea or something in the cafeteria and she would come and meet me in like an hour to tell me what was going on.

So I've been here for like two hours. And she did say she would come. And my mum sent a text to Carol. She was on her way in anyway and she's gone to meet Malin as soon as she can find him. And I sent a text to a lady at Sarah's work to say that maybe she was waking up so they should send a tape of their voices or something. And I thought I could go to Sarah's and get her some clothes cos she won't wanna wear that blue gown thing when she wakes up, will she? I can get her that big purple scarf that she loves. And I think I'll have another Coke.

Mr Malin has just walked into the cafeteria. It's late now and no one else is here. The cafe shut like half an hour ago and there's just the hum and glow of the vending machine for company. But Malin is here and Beth is walking in behind him. My mum is there too. And Carol. They all look too serious. WTF. She's fucking waking up and they're not even pleased.

Malin is dragging the plastic chair out from under the table. The legs drag on the floor.

'Kelly,' he says, in that fake-caring, patronising, I'm-older-and-smarter-than-you-are twatty voice that he has. 'Kelly, I'm really sorry. Sarah is not waking up.'

'You weren't there, Mr Malin. You weren't fucking there. You didn't see. She moved her eyes. She's fucking waking up, I know it.'

Beth put her arm around me.

'You know she moved her eyes, Beth. Tell him she moved her eyes.' I can feel sick coming up my throat. I am so hot. They are so fucking stupid.

'Kelly, what you saw is misleading. I'm so sorry.'

'You weren't fucking there, you twat.'

'Jesus, Mary and Joseph, Kelly! Will you not speak to the doctor like that.'

'Mum, you weren't there. She moved her eyes. She could see my hand.'

'Kelly, I'm afraid that it's a common involuntary reflex response to motion that you witnessed. It's not a voluntary response. Do you understand? Sarah is in a persistent vegetative state right now. That's what we see on the brain scans and on all the other tests. You need to understand that Sarah is not aware of anything. There is no high brain function at all. I wish there were. We will keep monitoring her though, Kelly. We will keep hoping that she will come through. But you have to prepare yourself for the worst outcome. We all do.'

He is looking around at all of us. In the light from the vending machine his face is glowing green. He could be in a horror movie.

My mum is standing up. She's still lugging that cassette player around.

'C'mon, Kelly. Time to go home. Thanks for coming down, Mr Malin. Beth. It means a lot to us.'

There's a pain in my stomach. I'm going to be sick. They're starting to walk away. My mum is doing up her coat.

They're giving up on Sarah.

Carol is collecting up the Coke cans and putting them on a tray.

They're gonna let Sarah die when she's not dead. Beth is staring at me.

'She was awake!' Malin's heels are making tap-tap-tapping noises on the tiled floor like a girl's. 'I saw her!' My mum has got hold of my arm. The pain in my stomach is getting worse. 'She looked in my fucking eyes.'

Sarah's sister is looking in her bag and Beth has said something but I can't hear it. The fucking bastards don't know her like I do. Carol's staring at me too.

'She was my best friend.'

The pain is getting higher in my stomach.

She wasn't supposed to fucking die.

It's crawling up my chest.

I think I'm going to faint.

It's so hot.

They are liars.

He's a fucking liar.

He's a fucking stupid fucking liar stupid bastard stupid ...

A scream.

A high-pitched fucking scared fucking nightmare scream.

Malin has turned around and is running back towards us with his white coat flying open. The scream is getting louder and louder. My mum is trying to grab hold of my arm. She's shouting. I can feel her breath on my face. Beth has got hold of my shoulders.

More screaming.

Beth's saying, 'Look at me, Kelly. Look at me, Kelly.'

It's so hot and the scream just keeps screaming and screaming.

'Look at me, Kelly. Look at me, Kelly.'

There's a crack as a hand hits my cheek.

Slap.

Stop.

Quiet.

45

Sarah

Day Ten – 1 a.m.

'The brother's been arrested again.'

Lucinda is whispering over my bed.

'What, Adam's brother?'

She's on with Lisa.

'No, David Cameron's brother!'

'Who?'

'Jesus Christ, Lisa. How did you ever pass your medical exams? Yes, Adam's brother.'

'Ash?'

'Yes, your special friend Ash. He'd stolen a load of money. Fifty thousand pounds. Turns out he'd given it to Adam to look after. Adam knew all about it. Sarah didn't. Well, they think she didn't. He was coming in here to try to get it back. The police caught him ransacking the house. He didn't find it. It was at the bottom of a box in the back of a cupboard. Hidden under a pile of porn magazines. He'd taken up half the floorboards.'

'People are so weird. Why do you always act like I'm thick?'

This means nothing to me. I remember hearing about Ash but I never met him. He was always in trouble. Running up bills in hotels and not paying them. Fifty thousand pounds.

I'm trying to remember if Adam had said anything about Ash recently but to be honest I can't really remember much of the past month. Not since Liverpool.

My sister has arrived.

'Listen to this, Mum.'

And my mother. They've come back.

'What is it, Carol?'

Did I tell you I thought I saw Kelly? I did. I saw Kelly. I'm sure of it. I'm getting better. I'm actually gonna get out of here.

'It's a leaflet that Gill gave Dad, you know, the support lady. The really, really annoying one.'

'Gill Brannon has been nothing but kind to us. She even paid for our train fare.'

The light was so bright.

'It's a hospice leaflet. "Process-Oriented Hospice Care". It's "psychotherapeutic work with patients, families and professionals in the middle of near-death experiences including comatose, vegetative and other highly withdrawn states of consciousness".'

'I don't think that really refers to us, Carol, thank you.'

'Seriously, Mum. You are going to have to get real at some point.'

What?

'What your mother means is that there are still many options open to us. We aren't giving up on Sarah.'

'I don't think, Mum, that you –'

'Please don't patronise your mother.'

'I'm not fucking patronising anyone. This is the fucking real world here.'

'If you are going to use that language –'

'Dad, listen. It's not what you think. It says –'

'I don't care what it says. You're just upsetting everyone, as usual. You're so bloody-minded. You always have been. You are talking about my daughter here. Your sister. This is not the way that life is supposed to go. You don't bury your own child. You don't bring life into the –'

He's crying. I'm crying.

'Dad, stop. I know. Please stop. Let me read this. According to this bloke, Posner or something, "A patient who appears non-communicative may still experience the world around them and is capable of communicating using subtle, often barely detectable nonverbal signals." You see?'

'What is she saying, Brian?'

'"Patients in comatose states have traditionally been considered by mainstream medicine to be victims of pathological processes that curtail normal cognitive and communicative functioning. Modern research suggests that patients may display 'islands' of consciousness in even persistent vegetative states."'

'What is she talking about, Brian?'

'I'm saying that Sarah may be awake some of the time, just not all of the time. She may have islands of being able to hear us, understand us.'

Islands? Yes, islands. That's what it is.

'It says, "The range of comatose and vegetative states described by medicine are thought to be without intrinsic meaning, and the experiences of their victims without significance. Since, by definition, the patient is incapable of understanding, thinking about or communicating about his or her own condition, this view precludes the participation of patients in their own care." It says, "Coma work allows patients to become active participants in their own care.""

Their own care? What does that mean?

'"Coma work begins with the attitude that the comatose patient is capable of perceiving and relating to outer and inner experience, no matter how minimally. The coma worker therefore tries to discover what communication channels are open to the patient, and then to use these channels to relate to the patient's experience. Channels of communication may be identified by noticing small, sometimes minute signals in the form of movement, eye movement, facial expressions and vocalisation by the patient. The coma worker then attempts to interact with the patient by interacting with and amplifying these signals." Fuck, why have the doctors not been doing any of this? Where the fuck is Malin? He needs to do all this coma work stuff!'

The door opens.

'This all looks very serious. What's going on? Hello, Mum and Dad. Glad to see you're here. How are we all today?'

Beth is back.

'Look, I know you all want to be here, but right now I've got jobs that need to be done. Why don't you all go and get a coffee or something? The cafeteria is open.'

'We were actually hoping to talk to Mr Malin. We've been reading up on this coma work thing. Do you know anything about it?'

'The place in St John's Wood? I know a few patients who've moved there.'

'And did they ... you know – did they get better?'

'You should make an appointment to see them. They are really nice people.'

'But did they get better?'

'Mrs Beresford, I'll be honest. It's not what Process-Oriented Hospice Care is about. You don't go there to get better. You go there when there are few opportunities left to you. The idea is that if the patient has some way of communicating then they can make some decisions about their future.'

'I think we'd all prefer her to just get better, actually, Beth. But thank you.'

You know in a film or a book or something someone says they are frozen with fear, well, I am frozen with fear. It's not that I'm cold. I can't feel anything. It's not even that I can't move, though obviously I can't. It's like my thoughts have seized up. Malin was just in. He was here with Beth. He told all the people that I care about, my family, he told them all basically to switch off the life support. He's not actually going to do it himself. He says it's time for them to consider it. Them! I don't have a choice in the matter. He wants to take me off life support and let nature take its course. He actually said that. LET NATURE TAKE ITS COURSE.

My Dad is here with Carol and my mother. They came back because he told them they had to make a decision. The decision is whether or not to switch off my life support. Whether or not to kill me.

And all the time he was talking, all I could think about was: why isn't he actually doing some work rather than standing around pontificating about my fucking quality of fucking life? Shouldn't he be doing tests or something? Should he be organising MRI scans? Is that all he's got to do?

My mother is crying. My dad is fussing over her, making sure she's taken her tablets and insisting that they go back to the Travelodge. Brenda is here too, talking to the nurses about Kelly. Kelly isn't here, I don't think.

They've all gone now. All I can hear is the buzz, click, hum of my life being supported. For how much longer?

What's weird is that I was feeling so much better today. So far out of the deep hole of nothingness. I actually dreamt I saw Kelly at one point. It felt so real. For like five seconds I saw her face, crystal clear. Her green eyes gazing into mine. Her hand moving close to my face. I could have sworn it was real. It can't have been.

46

Kelly

I've already been into school. It's Monday morning. Mum was still asleep when I crept out of the front door. She was up most of the night with me. I lost the day yesterday. I just slept. Half of me thought if I left Sarah alone she might prove everyone wrong and wake up. But she didn't. My mum spent the day paranoid. I kept waking up to find her right in front of me, just staring at my face. She made me a fish-finger sandwich. She must've thought I'd lost my mind. When I asked her, she dyed my hair for me, back to White Platinum, and ironed it straight, like Clare used to. She would've done anything to calm me down.

Billy was up early, but he didn't see me leave. He was too busy watching CBeebies – some naff cartoon. The road was silent and the High Street weirdly empty. The usual tide of commuters going to the tube hadn't started. No one else was around, really, apart from the night workers coming back the other way. The school run hadn't begun. There was fog in the air and my breath was coming out in little clouds. My lungs hurt. I tried not to run even though I wanted to. I tried to walk slow, like I had not much to do, no fucking place to go. I had a hoody, a beanie, my satchel, my old school shoes and an empty sports bag. The rest of me was as plain as you fucking like. Dull Kelly. Dumb little schoolgirl Kelly. Stupid skirt, nasty shoes. Colourless latex gloves. The last pair in the pack. I detoured past the bus shelter, no one around. No CCTV in operation. Gum still in place. On to the bench. Grab the bat. Shove it in the sports bag. Through the car park by the Rec. The trees lost and silent in the grey fog.

I took the art-block entrance in Grove Road as usual. I walked up the alleyway by the bike sheds where clumps of Clare's hair were once stuck along the gutter of the redbrick wall. I turned into the dining-hall block. There was a guy polishing the parquet floor with one of them floor-polishing machines. He had headphones on. He didn't look up. The locker room is at the end of the dining hall. It has a swing door. The lights weren't on. I didn't need lights. I knew where I had to go, what I had to do. I emptied most of the contents of my satchel and the sports bag into the locker and closed it using the pink padlock key.

I left the locker room and headed for the girls' toilets, the ones next to the bike sheds. The guy had got about three metres further up the parquet floor. Headphones still on. It looked fucking fun, that floor polishing. I want a go.

The windows in the girls' loos are at the top of the walls and flip open outwards, and if you stand on the back of the toilet you can just see out. I took off the hoody and beanie. I had a hairbrush and a hairband in the side pocket of my satchel. I bent forwards and brushed my hair upside down so I could get the highest ponytail possible, a My Little fucking Pony ponytail, then

I dropped the brush on the tiled floor and twisted the hair into the band. I checked in the mirror. I pulled up my collar, brushed on my glittery lip gloss in Pepto-Bismol pink, turned over the waistband of my skirt twice and rolled my socks over my knees, like stockings. My wedges were in my satchel. Shabby little tart. I could hear the sound of bicycles and voices so I climbed onto the toilet seat to look out. Alex Hall, Wino, Tom Bush and Rob Long were sitting with their backs against the wall of the bike sheds – their usual spot to meet Kathryn. The early shift. They were making rollies, eyeing up victims. A small kid arrived on a too-big bike. It must've been new. His blazer sleeves were over his hands. He must have used an entire pot of hair gel to get his quiff. It was solid. He wiped his nose on the length of his sleeve, like little kids do, and examined it. Alex nodded towards him and Rob sneered that fucking weird sneer he does. Like a fucking animal. The kid was like totally not knowing what he had walked into. He got his fucking phone out of his fucking blazer pocket and polished the screen on his lapel. He unstrapped his laptop case from the back of his bike (for fuck's sake – he may as well have a sign) and searched in his blazer pockets. He yanked out a pair of canary-yellow headphones and while he balanced his bike against his leg he pushed the headphones into his ears. One popped out. He stared at it like he was not quite sure what it was, then he pushed it back in his ear. He was humming. Behind him Wino, Rob and Alex were dragging on their roll-ups and starting to stand up. They started taunting him. 'Oy, kid. Got a hard hairstyle there, have you? Bit of a quiff like the big lads? Got a new phone there have you. Kid?'

He couldn't hear them.

I left the toilets in a hurry but I didn't forget anything. I checked. The empty sports bag I left under one of the sinks along with a load of other empty sports bags that had long been forgotten. I didn't need that again. And my own bag was in one of the cubicles. I doubled back to the other side of the bike sheds so that I could get into them from the art-block entrance – out of shadows. It was still totally dark from that direction. Wino, Rob and Tom had made a circle around the little kid and were pushing him, nicking stuff from his pockets as he went round and round. As I drew level with them they turned. I must have looked like a vague shadow in the darkness of the bike sheds. They stopped what they were doing. I drifted past, eyes forward, with just a few metres between us, separated by the bike-shed wall. The only thing they could've seen absolutely for sure was the platinum-white hair. In the high ponytail. No mistaking that hair. And no mistaking that swagger. And the fog was still hanging in the air. Thank God for fucking fog. I heard the sound of a bike fall and the little kid running. And a breathless 'What the fuck!'

In the girls' toilets I changed back. Back into the hoody and the beanie. Back to the shite shoes and the long skirt. I changed slowly, deliberately. I made no mistakes. I was the invisible me again. And the whole time in the toilets I could hear them shouting, arguing, fighting.

'It fucking was her!'

'You twat, it couldn't have been.'

'She's dead, fucker. Dead.'

'Even if she's not dead, you cut her hair off, you twat. It must be someone else.'

'It wasn't someone fucking else. It was her.'

'And that's a ghost come back to haunt you then, is it? Whoooooooaa.'

'Fuck off, Hall. Fuck off.'

'Twat.'

'Who are you calling a twat, fuckhead? Get over here and say that.'

There was the slap of skin meeting skin, bone meeting bone. Someone yelled.

'You fucking stabbed him, you cunt! You fucking stabbed him!'

There was groaning. Some girls started screaming.

As I walked out of the girls' toilets I saw over the bike-shed wall that Kathryn Cowell had already got involved in the fighting. She was shouting. People were running. Wino was dragging her by her coat. Wino dragging Kathryn Cowell. Someone shouted, 'Knife!' and Mrs Backhouse started running towards them while Miss Meering started dialling frantically on her phone.

And as I slowly made my way out of the art-block door on the back road to town, the police sirens were whining up the road leading to the front entrance. More vans flew past as I got to White Hart Lane.

I'm back at home now. Billy must've just gone to school. The remaining Honey Loops in his bowl have gone soggy in the milk. My mum has left a plate with a marmaladey knife on it, and a note on the side. It says, 'Hope you like your hair.'

She thinks I'm still in bed.

I'm going in to talk to Sarah.

47

Kelly and Sarah

Day Eleven – 11 a.m.

'They don't believe me. They said you didn't wake up. But you did, didn't you, Sarah?'

Kelly is here. Kelly. I can hear her. I saw her. I know I saw her.

'Still chatting away, Kelly? Well done. Oooh, nice hair.'

'Fuck off, Beth.'

'Pardon? Come on, Kelly. That's not like you.'

'What the fuck would you know, Nurse La-di-fucking-da? You dare to come in here now? Why don't you just go and fill out a fucking form or something? Leave me alone with her. I need to talk to her. I need to tell her something. Why are you fucking touching me? GET THE FUCK OUT OF HERE!'

Kelly, just calm down.

'I just wanted to –'

'Get the fuck off me –'

'I just wanted to tell you. Langlands. The Detective Inspector. He's coming. Here.'

'And? What the fuck does that mean?'

'He called. Really early this morning.'

Langlands is coming for her.

'So?'

'So he asked if you were here. Asked if I knew if you were coming. I said I didn't know.'

'And what's he gonna do? Tell the fucking school? Put me in prison for bunking off to see my sick friend? Do I give a fuck? No! Watch my lips. I DO NOT GIVE A FUCK. Not about him, not about you, not about your fucking common fucking involuntary reflex fucking response, not about ticking fucking boxes on your fucking forms. Guess what, Beth, I'm not even fucking lying. Do you get that?'

'He thinks ... he thinks you had something to do with all this.'

'Oh, right. Brilliant. Inspector Gadget strikes again. So now he's gonna pin it all on a schoolgirl, is he?'

Shut up, Kelly. Shut up.

'Kelly. You're not really what you pretend to be, are you?'

'Look, Nurse Hodder. I think you've done enough, don't you? You're the one who's been pretending. Pretending to be my BEST PAL and snitching the entire time to that scum policeman. What do you think? That I killed Adam? Really? A fourteen-year-old?'

'No, of course not, Kelly. I don't think that. At least, I don't think I think that ... I don't know ...'

She's crying. Beth is crying.

'Listen, Kelly, if I were you, I would go. Get out of here now. You can't do anything more for Sarah right now. Go to school.'

'I've been to school. Already. This morning. Seven a.m. To the locker room. Pink padlock. Pink fucking padlock. Fucking bat. Fucking locker. Fucking credit cards. Cash. IDs. Driving licences. All in the fucking locker, right? I can't go back there. Not now. If she finds that bat, Wino will work it all out. Two My Little fucking Pony blondes. She'll kill me.'

'What are you talking about? Who'll kill you? Kelly, you're scaring me …'

I can see Adam. I can see him. He's waiting outside the community centre. Where he always is. It's late. It's dark. He's leaning over, one hand on his knee, the other propped up on the lamp post. He's vomiting onto the pavement. As usual. As he does every week when I leave the centre after the mediation counselling. The mediation counselling he wouldn't come to.

'Kathryn Cowell will kill me.'

'Why would she kill you? You should tell Langlands. Kelly, you have to tell the police everything. If you don't, you're going to get into more trouble.'

I'm wearing latex gloves. I am staring at my hands in the dark and I have latex gloves on. And now there's a bat in my hand. It was hidden in the bushes by the bus shelter. And now it's in my hot and sweaty hands in the hot and sweaty gloves. And Adam is looking up the street. Trying to focus.

'Sarah is my best friend, my only friend. I can't do this without her. Sarah. Sarah! Wake the fuck up.'

And then he turns and looks right at me. Right in my eyes. And he's trying to focus. And he smiles. He sees the bat in my hand and he smiles. Like he knows I'm a coward and that I can't do what I'd planned to do. Because I'm nothing. No one. Just a dolly that he can manipulate. Just someone he can fuck whenever he feels like it. Because it is his conjugal right. That's what he always says. Conjugal right. CONJUGAL RIGHT. And I take a step forward. CONJUGAL RIGHT. And another step. CONJUGAL RIGHT. And I break into a run. And I stretch out my arm, and my arm is at full stretch and I arch out the bat in a circular motion and ... CONJUGAL RIGHT. There's a hollow heavy thud as the bat meets his temple – square on, right where the skull is at its flattest. Right where the victim is at his most vulnerable. Temple blow. He takes a step towards the lamp post. He pushes himself up. Trying to focus. Staring at me. And his legs buckle. And he crumples up. Forehead first. Cheek resting on the pavement. His soft cheek. Cold pavement. Grit. The cheek I used to kiss. A bubble of spit and sick and blood slides along his mouth. His soft mouth, I used to kiss. The bubble grows bigger. And pops. Pop. And it turns into a sticky drip of blood, a channel of blood that mixes into a small pool of rainwater on the ground. There's a pink-and-yellow lolly wrapper next to his hair. The hair I used to stroke. His eyes stare at me. Then cross. Then close. There's a girl standing next to him. A schoolgirl. Plain. In the shadows behind the bus shelter. She has gloves on too. Latex gloves like mine. She stares at the broken body on the pavement encircled by a pool of blood that's seeping along the gaps between the paving slabs. Then she calmly walks over and takes the bat out of my hand. And she turns quickly and leaps up to the bench and throws the bat onto the roof of the bus shelter. It clatters on the corrugated iron.

Then, fragile blood-bubbling silence.

'Excuse me, Nurse Hodder.'

She pulls the gloves off me. And puts them in her pocket. Then she takes out Adam's wallet and takes his card and ID and cash. And she takes my bag and opens my purse and takes my cards too. Then she throws the bag on the ground.

'C'mon, Sarah. C'mon. Don't fucking lose it now.'

She keeps telling me to trust her. To fall back. To do the trust fall. I can't move. I can't think. Kelly. What do I do? I spread out my arms. Wide. And wait for the friends to catch me. I can hear them laughing in my head. 'Come on, Sarah – you can trust us.' *But there are no friends there. Kelly whispers to me to fall back. Just fall back. Stick to the plan, Sarah. It has to look right,' she says. I am falling. Falling back. No hands to catch me.*

'Excuse me, Nurse Hodder. Excuse me, Nurse Hodder. There's a call about Kelly.'

Kelly.

'Lisa, can you just take a message for me? I just need to –'

'They said it was important. It's Kelly's mum.'

'Lisa, for once in your life can you handle it? Can't you see that I need some time here –'

'You go, Beth. Fuck off. Go on.'

Kelly.

'She said the police are at the school. There's been some kind of riot. That's what she said to say. She said they arrested someone. A few people. Someone got stabbed.'

'Lisa, for Christ's sake, can you tell them –'

'They've arrested a girl. Some girl. She had a bat in her locker. With blood on it. And the cards. And the cash.'

Reading Group Questions

• The two protagonists in *The Last Thing I Remember*, Sarah and Kelly, have such different voices. Which was your favourite?

• The voice of Kelly is very authentic. How do you think the author might have got into the head of a fourteen-year-old girl?

• Can you imagine what it must be like for Sarah – being able to hear what's going on around her, but being unable to communicate?

• What did you think of Kelly as a character? Do you think she's as strong as she likes to make out?

• Kelly comments on the fact that people always assume that you can tell who a person is from the way they present themselves and the clothes that they wear. How important do you think first impressions are when you meet someone, and how can the way we dress define our character?

• Why do you think Sarah wanted to help Kelly when she first met her, and how does the advice she gives to Kelly reflect her own situation?

- Bullying is an important theme in *The Last Thing I Remember*. Why do you think Kelly is bullied?

- Sarah's parents decided to ignore the trauma that happened to Sarah in her childhood. How damaging can it be to cover up secrets from the past, and can we ever really forget?

- Were you shocked by the twist at the end, or did you see it coming?

- Do you think Sarah was justified in her actions and who do you think is ultimately to blame?

Want to join the conversation? Let us know what you thought of the book online @BonnierZaffre #LastThingIRemember